OF DESTINY AND ILLUSIONS

Thunderbird Academy #2

VALIA LIND

OF DESTINY AND ILLUSIONS

THUNDERBIRD ACADEMY - BOOK TWO

Valia Lind

It is not in the stars to hold our destiny but in ourselves.

— WILLIAM SHAKESPEARE

This is the screw up of all screw ups. I have ruined everything. If they were giving out awards for the biggest mess-up of the century, I would be the recipient. Hands down.

I've been sitting in this room for what seems like hours. I haven't seen my friends or spoken to anyone since the Elders and Headmaster Marković were ushered into the Spring Court's private chambers. The large intricate design on the doors does nothing to minimize the fear I feel knowing they're in there, deliberating my future.

My mind drifts to my friends, and I really hope they're okay. If I'm being honest, I have no idea what my spell actually did. Sure, I went ahead and moved the whole school, including the outside campus, right into the middle of the Faery's forest. But that's all I know. My friends were out there, fighting the creatures sent by the Ancients. They could've gotten hurt. Or worse.

I really shouldn't think like that, but my mind is my worst enemy.

When the door finally opens, I think the Elders have come to banish me to some unknown plane of existence, but then Liam slips in.

"Maddie." He says my name softly and then he's across the room in a flash, pulling me out of the chair and into his arms. I grip him tightly, basking in the feel of the comfort he provides.

"I'm sorry," I whisper against his chest, and I feel him stiffen. He pulls away just a tad, glancing down into my face.

"You have nothing to be sorry about."

"Right, can you make sure you mention that to, oh I don't know, everyone?" I step out of his arms, frustration and fear once again ruling my body.

"Maddie, you did the best you could with the information you were given." I glance at him sharply and find that quiet wisdom on his face that I've missed so much. "If Headmaster Marković asked you to story cast, then he should've given you proper instruction."

"It's not like there was time."

"Then they should've found another way."

As he speaks, I realize something. He's angry. In the year I've known him, I don't think I've ever seen him angry. Fae are known for mastering their emotions. It takes a bit to get them rattled.

"Liam, what is it?"

"How are you feeling?" he asks instead, and I narrow my eyes.

"Liam." At first, I think he'll continue beating around the bush, but he surprises me.

"Maddie, story spell casting is dangerous. Especially for the witch who wields the power. How are you feeling?"

"I'm fine, honestly. I felt drained the first time I did it. But not so much now."

My words don't seem to reassure him in the least. He studies me like I'm a bug under a microscope, and I shift foot to foot under the scrutiny. Now that he mentions it, I do feel more tired than I initially thought. But I'm not about to tell him that. It's just the adrenaline wearing off.

"Can you tell me what's happening in there?" I ask instead, motioning toward the closed doors. Liam glances behind him, and I swear his look just got a tad darker. But when he turns back to me, I find no trace of that fleeting emotion.

"You rattled quite a few cages, Maddie." He sighs, taking my hand and leading me toward the love seat positioned under the large window. It's opposite from the doors. I've been trying to stay away from it, if only to keep myself from staring outside and freaking myself out more than I already am.

"I didn't mean to."

"No, but what's done is done." Liam doesn't let go of my hand as we sit, and I'm grateful for the small comfort his skin offers mine. We've never been touchy feely before, but I think he realizes I need this right now. I'm teetering at the edge, overwhelmed by the knowledge of what I've done, of what I'm capable of. It's not an easy burden to carry.

"What do you think will happen next?" I'm not sure I'm ready for the answer, but I need it all the same.

"I think they will ask you to write a spell to take the school back to the human realm. But I'm not sure how effective that will be."

"What do you mean?" It takes him a long time to reply, but I don't push. Something is going on here, and it's up to him to share whatever he deems best. When he finally speaks, it's not what I expect.

"The Ancients are right on the border of Faery, Maddie." His words are heavy with everything he's not saying. "I know everyone thinks this place is impenetrable, but the Ancients' magic is stronger than anything we've ever encountered. And they're getting through. Somehow they're getting through."

This time, I'm the one who offers an encouraging squeeze to his hand, and he grips it tightly. I thought him staying home would keep him safe. Instead, it put him in even more danger.

"Do you think they'll get through?"

"We are not about to let that happen."

The voice comes from our right, and both Liam and I jump to our feet as I turn to watch a group of people walk through the doors. The woman at the front can only be described as strikingly gorgeous. Her porcelain skin and platinum blonde hair glow brightly enough to light up the space around her. Her crystal blue eyes are on me, her lips rosy, as if she's wearing makeup. Except I know better. I'm mesmerized by her, and I can't help it.

"Your Highness," Liam bows beside me, and I hurry to follow suit. So, this is the High Queen of Spring Court. Stories about her do not do her justice. Even her gown is more intricate than I would've imagined. The color is of blooming buds on a spring day, and it seems to flow around her as if it's dancing in the wind.

"Madison Hawthorne." The queen speaks, her eyes piercing me right through. "You have created quite a predicament. What do you have to say for yourself?"

"I'm not a very good storyteller?" I shrug, and for a second, I think she might actually smile. "I'm sorry, Your Highness."

"Do not ever apologize for your power, child." She waves a hand, as if waving away my words. "Come, we have much to discuss."

The headmaster meets my eye over the queen's shoulder with an encouraging smile on his face. I have no idea how I got myself into this mess, but as I trail after the queen, I realize, I will do whatever it takes to turn this into my greatest victory.

After all, I am a Hawthorne. I have a legacy to live up to and an opportunity to create my own.

❧

WE DON'T GO BACK INTO THE CHAMBERS, OR WHATEVER THAT room actually is, behind the closed doors. Instead, the queen leads us outside. I'm too nervous to appreciate the gorgeous castle walls and the beautiful art displayed all around me. My heart feels like it's going to beat right out of my chest. The headmaster, Liam and two of the Elders, Matilda included, are walking a few steps behind me.

Once outside, I take a deep breath, inhaling the freshness of the perpetual springtime. I've never visited Faery before, but it's always been a dream of mine. Especially after I met Liam. I glance back at him, and he gives me a tiny smile of encouragement. He's unlike any fae I've ever read about, his kindness toward me has always come first. But I have no misconceptions about the beautiful creature walking in front of me. The queen would have me killed in a second if it fancied her.

"Madison Hawthorne," When the queen speaks, I understand why songs are sung about fae's ability to draw in humans with just one word. My name sounds like a lyrical poem on her lips. "Look around. What do you see?"

"The school?" Because there it is, situated amongst the tallest trees I have ever seen, Thunderbird Academy stands completely untouched by the effects of my spell. Except for *where* it's standing.

"What do you know about the story casting you performed?" She turns to glance at me, and I feel that look root me to the ground. The rest of our entourage feels miles away as I stare at the gorgeous creature in front of me.

"I'm afraid I don't know much. I never thought I would use it."

"But then you used it twice."

Confusion must be plain on my face because I have no idea how she could know such a thing. Unless the headmaster told her. Actually, I take it back. It was probably Elder Matilda. She's out to get me; I know that for a fact. But then, the queen surprises me with a laugh. It sounds like the first rainfall of spring beating on tender leaves. The sound pulls me in until I don't want to listen to anything else.

"I can see the magic on you, Madison Hawthorne. You almost reek of it."

That snaps me back to reality. I glance down, as if I would be able to see the physical effect of my magic, but of course there's nothing. It takes me a full minute before I can bring myself to look at the queen again. I need to be more careful and not be so mesmerized by her presence. Even though it's difficult, it's possible. My sister's best friend is dating one of the fae from the Spring

Court, and I, of course, asked Nolan enough questions to become annoying. Now I'm glad that I have.

When I finally meet the queen's eye, she gives me a cold smile.

"There is knowledge in your eyes, Madison Hawthorne." I have no idea how to take that, so I don't respond. "But there is also immaturity to your magic. You have broken through the Vale in the most unconventional way, which puts the whole realm in danger."

There is not a hint of kindness in her voice, and it chills me to the bone. I don't want to show fear, so I solidify my resolve as much as possible. I'm not sure it helps any, but I don't back down.

"Tomorrow, you are to come see me for a ...conversation." I try not to show the shock I'm feeling, but I doubt I succeed. "That is all."

She doesn't wait for a response but leaves me standing as she turns and walks back into the castle. I'm so flabbergasted, I don't even have it in me to bow. Once she's gone, Liam is by my side, along with the headmaster and Elder Matilda.

"Now you have gone and done it," she hisses at me. "The Queen of the Spring Court is not a fae you want on your bad side, so you better not mess it up."

"I don't understand." I finally find my voice, completely ignoring the woman and looking at my headmaster instead. "What does she want with me?"

"Miss Hawthorne, you..." He stops for a second, as if looking for the right words. "You are a fascinating subject for her, one she plans to study. I am afraid your attendance is required as it is one of the stipulations for us to stay here as free folk."

"You mean, she would put us in prison if I don't go to the meeting?"

"You are correct. The queen is not to be trifled with in any way. This may be the Spring Court, but do not have any misconceptions about the fact that you are in Faery."

He's right. The Spring Court may be one of the nicer ones in Faery, but that doesn't change anything. I let that sink in, my blood cold in my veins. I made everything so much worse. I wish I never would've opened my big mouth. Liam steps closer to me but doesn't offer empty words of encouragement. I'm in big trouble.

"What do we do now?" I ask, looking over my shoulder at Thunderbird Academy, my home away from home.

"Now, we learn all we can about your magic, resume school as usual, and train you to write a spell that will take us home."

"School?" I twist around, not sure I heard him correctly.

"Ah, yes. Unfortunately for us, your spell was a one-way ticket. With the Ancients right on the border, we cannot allow any students back into the human realm. Not yet. So, we are to go about our days, business as usual."

At first, I can't wrap my mind around his words. I thought I'd be the one to stay here and everyone else would be able to leave. To go home or go into hiding. This was going to be my punishment and no one else's.

"Are you saying we're stuck here?"

"That is precisely what I'm saying."

With those words, my already upside-down world completely shatters. Not only have I made myself the queen's personal guinea pig, but I sentenced my friends—and the entire school—to a stint in the Faery Realm. Against their will.

I hope they're okay. I doubt any of them will want to talk to me once they find out.

❦ 2 ❧

Thunderbird Academy cannot be more than half a mile away, but for some reason, it seems unreachable. Head-master and Elder Matilda have moved farther away, but I can still hear them arguing behind my back. Well, it's mostly Elder Matilda yelling at Headmaster Marković. Not that any of this is his fault. It's mine. I know it. The queen knows it. Everyone knows it.

"How are you holding up, cupcake?" I groan at the hated nick-name, turning just a bit to see Liam's grin.

"You're the cupcake, cupcake," I reply, our standard exchange. Honestly, I can't even remember how this started, but it became our thing. He's trying to make me feel better, but I don't.

"I really need you to get that chip off your shoulder, Maddie," the fae sighs. "We already discussed how this is not your fault."

"You say that because you're my friend."

"I say that because fae can't lie."

I glance at him then, noticing the seriousness that has entered his voice. So often, I forget he is not of my world. He's got that breathtaking glow about him that makes it difficult to stare for too long. It's like looking at the sun. But there is also kindness about him that's not typical to the fae. I know he's spent much of his years in the human world, despite his standing within the court. Even in his dark jeans, faded t-shirt, and leather jacket, he looks like royalty. That's when I realize he's dressed in human clothes.

"Why are you wearing that?" I ask, completely distracted now. He glances down at himself, as if realizing it for the first time.

"I had an errand to run."

"In the human realm?" My mind automatically goes to my family. Liam's half-brother is dating my sister's best friend. Wow, that's a mouthful. But it's also a link. "Have you seen my family?"

He shifts his eyes to the side, as if to see who is listening. When he turns back, I know he's not saying anything. Not here or right now.

"It was official business for the queen," he replies, and I nod my head in understanding, even as I try not to feel disappointed. Everything Liam does is calculated. It has always been so, and I know he won't put me in any kind of danger. Even when it comes to information. Yet, I still wish he would give me some kind of an indication.

As if reading all this in my face, Liam takes a step toward me, reaching for my arm. His hand wraps around my wrist, giving it the tiniest of squeezes, and I feel better instantly. Just then, Headmaster Marković comes up, and Liam drops my arm quickly. I don't have to be reminded that my friendship with Liam has always been a bit of a sore spot for his family. But now that his family reconciled with his brother, I wonder if that has changed. Just another question among the millions of questions I want to ask him when we're alone.

"We should get back to the school," Headmaster says, and I look over his shoulder to see Elder Matilda disappearing back into the castle.

"Is Elder Matilda not coming?" I ask.

"No, the Elders have much to discuss," Headmaster replies, his eyes on the school. I can't quite read his features, but he almost looks sad to me. "I am sorry for putting you in this position, Miss

Hawthorne," he says, and now his expression makes sense. He feels guilty. Well, get in line.

"It's not your fault."

"Oh, but it is. If I had thought this through, instead of jumping to the first plausible solution, we might not be in this mess."

"Or it would've been a worse kind of a mess," I reply, looking him straight in the eye. "You didn't make me perform a spell. I did that all on my own."

"Yet, I am your headmaster. It is my job to guide you in the ways of magic."

"Not that I'm not enjoying this blame ping pong," Liam interrupts, taking a step forward. "The only party responsible are the Ancients. They were the ones who invaded Thunderbird Academy. They are the ones who should carry the blame. What you need to do is use the knowledge you have gained and make sure next time will be better."

Headmaster and I stare at Liam in silence as I let those words sink in. He's right, of course. But it's the way he says it that really gets to me. There's complete faith in his eyes and behind his words. He believes we can do this, that *I* can do this. I can't let him down. I can't let any of them down.

"I really missed you, Liam," I say, and the fae flashes me one of his heart-stopping grins.

"I know."

৩৫৩

WHEN WE GET BACK TO THE ACADEMY, THE PLACE IS EERILY quiet. A part of me expected chaos. I should really stop expecting anything at this point. My life isn't exactly anything I would've planned for myself.

Headmaster leads the way toward the large auditorium with Liam and me trailing behind. The fae's eyes keep darting around the area, as if he's waiting for something to jump out at us. It's never been my nature to be paranoid, but I'm rethinking that stand with the current events. Taking a step closer to Liam, I lower my voice and ask, "Should I be looking for something?"

He looks over at me, flashing me one of his quick smiles before replying.

"Nothing in particular. But you're in my world now, so I would advise you to always be looking for something."

Cryptic, but that's fae for you. As we continue walking, a low buzzing sound seems to come from the walls, but I can't pinpoint it. So instead I focus on my friend.

After meeting Liam last year, I did a lot of sneaky research to learn more about his kind. Before him, I never even imaged I would meet one. My hometown hasn't had a fae resident in generations. Not until Liam's half-brother, Nolan, came to stay there. If there is a lesson I remember from my childhood, it's the hierarchy of danger my mother taught me about. Shifters are at the top of that list. But what tops even them are the fae folk. One misplaced word and you can be indebted to them for a lifetime.

Not that I ever had to worry about that with Liam. Although, I'm still cautious. He even tells me to be. And like he said, fae can't lie. It doesn't matter what I think of his people, I'm just glad he's here. The feeling of dread hasn't gone away, and I fear that whatever the headmaster is about to tell the students will be just as earth shattering to me.

"Miss Hawthorne." The headmaster turns as we reach the double doors leading to the auditorium. "Please stay at the back of the stage for the time being."

"I'll stay with her." Liam immediately speaks up while I'm still trying to figure out why he's keeping me in the background. The headmaster gives my friend an affirmative nod before he pulls the doors open and steps inside. We follow close behind, but while he continues to the stage, Liam pulls me to a stop. "Give him a minute."

"Why?"

"Because, by the sound of it, people are not happy."

That's when I realize, the low buzz I've been hearing are

people's voices talking over each other in the next room. I creep toward the stage, keeping to the shadows, and I feel Liam's presence at my back. There is unmistakable panic in people's voices, even some animal growls and chirps. That tells me some of the shifters are in so much emotional distress, they can't control their shift.

"Please settle down," Headmaster's voice booms, amplified by magic to be heard in the farthest corners of the room. Everyone quiets instantly, and I wish I could see inside. But we're behind a large curtain, keeping as still as we can. There are plenty of shifters in the room that can sniff me out if I make even a little bit of a noise.

"I understand you are all scared," Headmaster Marković continues, his voice soothing and authoritative at the same time. "Queen Amaryllis has kindly opened up her land as a safe haven for our school. Since the Ancients have overrun our own grounds, I am sad to say, we will not be returning any time soon."

A murmur goes through the room at his words, and my own heart pangs painfully at the thought. I don't care what Liam says, I feel responsible for this outcome. Maybe if I was a better spell caster, I would've done a better job protecting us. Maybe if I was as strong or as smart as my sisters, I would've known my own limitations. No matter what anyone says, this is something I will have to live with. I just hope my actions haven't hurt anyone more than I already know they have.

"The grounds of Thunderbird Academy are protected, and while we are here, it will be business as usual. We will hold classes, we will train, and we will do what it takes to find a way back to our own way of life."

The murmur is much louder now, but I can't shake the feeling that Headmaster Marković is not telling us something vital.

"Since we are on Queen Amaryllis' land, she has asked for some of her court to be allowed to attend classes here. We will adjust accordingly. Now, please report to your rooms and further instructions will be given. Dismissed."

The headmaster doesn't allow for questions. He walks off the stage as soon as he says the words. I can hear the student body shouting at him for more information, but I know he won't provide it. Something else is happening here, and when the headmaster walks by where Liam and I are hiding, I take a step in front of him to block his path.

"What are you not telling them?" I ask, keeping my voice extra low in case any of the shifters can hear me. The headmaster looks me in the eye, and at first, I think he won't answer. But then, it's as if he's resigned to the fact that I need this information. When he opens his mouth, he looks older than I've ever seen him.

"Do not think for even a moment that we are guests here, Miss Hawthorne," Headmaster says, deliberately not looking in Liam's direction. "We have no way out and no choice but to obey. We are bound to this place for the time being, Miss Hawthorne. Please keep that knowledge to yourself."

"So, what you said before about me going to the meetings, it's much more than that. We're already prisoners."

He doesn't wait for a response, leaving me standing in the shadowed room, gaping at his retreating back.

"Stuck?" I turn to Liam, as the fae takes a step toward me. "We're stuck here?"

ৡ 3 ঽ

"**I** need to go see my friends," I announce. My mind is on Jade, who's probably full-on panicked by now at my absence. I think of Vera, Noel, Ben...and yes, even Aiden. They're my tribe, my people, and they probably think I've abandoned them. At least Kate is not here to be part of the mess. I just hope she's safe with her family. One day, when all of this is over, I'll find her and we'll catch up on all the things we missed about each others lives. But for now, I have to focus on what's right in front of me.

"I should get back to the castle. Will you be okay?"

Nodding my head is all I can do because, even though I know Liam has my back, a seed of doubt has been sown.

"Maddie." He takes a step closer, peering down into my face, and I have no choice but to look up. I'm blinded by his beauty once more, and I hate that I can't read anything in his eyes. "Everything will work out as it should."

"I like how you made sure to not say everything will be okay." I sigh, but this is just the way of their world. Words have power and when you can't lie, every single one is that much more powerful. Liam smiles at my observation but doesn't correct me.

"Your queen will really keep us here?"

"I told you, Maddie. We're at war. If she believes this is the best way, then that is what needs to be done."

"Even if we become prisoners?"

"We're all imprisoned one way or the other."

I glance at him sharply, surprised by the emotions brewing under that statement.

"We can sit around and be miserable. Or we can make the best out of a crappy situation."

It's difficult not to get inspired by his words. He's always had a way of getting right to the core of things and bringing them to a different light.

"You haven't lost your pep talk skills," I say now, flashing him a quick smile, "This is number five or six since I got here."

"It's what I do," he replies, bowing a little. Suddenly, I want to reach over and pull him into a hug because his arms will make me feel safe. If only for a moment. When we first found the library last year, we spent so much time together, I often forgot there are boundaries between our kind.

I squash the desire before I can take it any further. Maybe in the quiet of the secret library we could be something to each other, but here, in the light of day, we're a witch and a fae and there are eyes on us. No matter how much I have missed my friend, I have to remember where I am. I have to remind myself that I can stand on my own two feet.

"I'll come check on you later." Liam inclines his head before turning on his heels and walking away. After taking a few deep breaths, I make my way to the hallway.

There are a few students here and there, but not enough to make me nervous. No one pays me any more attention than usual, and I wonder if anyone knows what actually happened when the Ancients attacked. If they know I was directly involved.

But when no one starts throwing magic at me, I breathe a little easier and hurry to the staircase that leads me to my floor. There are even fewer people up here, most already safe in the confines of their rooms. No one seems to dare disobey Headmaster's instructions.

Jade is the first to see me. She freezes for half a second before she launches herself at me. I meet her halfway as she throws her arms around me, holding me tightly.

"Oh my gosh, I thought you were dead! I was so worried. We've been so worried. Those creatures seemed to descend out of nowhere, and we did our best, and then suddenly, we weren't there anymore, and the sky looked different, and where have you been?" She pulls back, breathing heavily as she takes me in, head to toe.

"I'm sorry to worry you," I reply, squeezing her hand briefly. "I was with the headmaster."

Thankfully, I don't get to say anything more as the rest of my friends reach us. I get pulled into a hug by Noel, nearly taking me off my feet, before I'm transferred to Vera. Even the hawk shifter seems to be showing an unusual amount of emotion as she gives me a quick hug. Then, I realize Ben is there, and even though he doesn't move to hug me, he gives me the kind of look that goes right through me. There's so much happiness and relief on his face, it almost brings tears to my eyes.

"Please head to your rooms immediately." The robotic voice sounds suddenly, making us all jump. "The lockdown is in full effect. Please head to your rooms immediately."

The rest of the hallway clears within seconds. My friends are reluctant to leave, and now that they see I'm safe, it's probably out of curiosity. Vera waves in our direction, heading off toward her room alone, and I realize she's the most affected by Christie's betrayal. She no longer has a roommate.

The boys are next to leave, after a long searching look at us. Just before Ben heads off, he moves toward me, touching my arm gently.

"I'm glad you're okay, Maddie," he whispers, his eyes intense on mine. "Aiden will be too." Then he's gone before I can interpret what he means by that. Jade takes my hand and pulls me toward our room as the last of the announcement sounds through the now empty hallway. The door shuts behind us and then we're alone.

I lean against the wood, my focus on breathing in deeply and exhaling fully. It feels like my heart rate has been at an all-time high since the moment I realized what I'd done.

"Are you okay?" Jade asks, and I open my eyes to find her sitting on her bed, her attention on me. She looks just as scared as I feel on the inside, so I push away from the door and walk toward her. Once seated, I turn to face her, trying to figure out what to say.

"Are *you* okay?" I ask, instead of answering.

"Honestly, I'm terrified. I know we've been training for battle since school began, but I never imagined it would come to this. And now, we're in Faery. Faery! You need a special invitation and a visa to visit, yet now we're living here. I don't know how to wrap my mind around that."

I can feel the panic creeping into her voice the longer she talks, and I truly wish Bri was here to offer some wisdom. My oldest sister is the best in these types of situations. But I can't seem to come up with anything because all I can think of is how it's my fault we ended up in this situation, and I can't even tell her that.

"We'll be okay, Jade," I say instead, giving her shoulder a little reassuring rub. I'm trying to convince myself as well as her.

"That's what people say when they don't think things will be okay."

"Let's not panic," I try again. I don't want to offer her empty promises, but I have to believe we will come out of this. "I say that because I believe it's possible and because that's the goal. We can and we will be okay, Jade."

She watches me for a long moment, as if searching the weight of my words. Finally, she leans her head on my shoulder and sighs.

"I hope my family is safe. I hope Headmaster finds a way to contact them. I can't imagine what they must be thinking."

It's a good point, but a moot one at the moment. My mind

drifts to my own family but only for a second. I can't focus on what I can't control. I already have plenty on that list.

"I'm sure they're safe. And since we've been on minimal communication, maybe they're not worried." Yet. I don't say it, but I don't have to. Jade understands.

"Yeah," Jade sighs again, sitting up. "I can't believe Christie would do this. She was our friend. How could she?"

I've been thinking about this at the back of my mind since she let the creatures into that building. Typically, there isn't a way to truly rationalize someone's actions because they have their own motivations. Always. But in this case, she told us what she wanted.

"Power can corrupt, and I think Christie just wanted it so badly, she didn't think about anything else."

"Like us."

"Yes, like us." I push down the sadness and the disappointment as I stand. "But you know what? That's on her. We did everything right. And we will continue to do so."

Jade gives me a brilliant smile, and I think I helped. In silence, we begin making preparations for bed and tomorrow. With the fae now walking the halls and controlling our every move, this will be the strangest school year. I just hope I don't accidentally send us somewhere worse.

Tomorrow, I will start looking for answers about my powers. Tomorrow, I will figure out how to play this game with the queen. For now, I rest and hopefully, my dreams won't be filled with a certain shifter, who apparently sent his beta to check on me.

THERE IS NO REPRIEVE IN SLEEP FOR ME. I TOSS AND TURN SO much, I end up wrapped in the blanket so tight, I smack myself in the face trying to get out. Some all-powerful witch I am. I tried slipping out to see if I could get to the greenhouse, but the doors are completely on lockdown. It seems this school has become our prison. At least for the time being.

The next morning, Jade and I wake up to a piece of paper being slipped under our door. She picks it up, glancing at it briefly before she walks over to me.

"What is it?"

"A list of things we can and cannot do." She sits beside me as we read, and the feeling of dread intensifies with each word.

"No leaving the premises without specific permission and an escort. Curfew is at exactly nine o'clock. Weekly dinners at the palace are not a negotiation. What's happening, Maddie?" Jade's voice rises in panic, and I reach over, placing my hand over hers.

"They're just rules, Jade. They're not a bad thing. Fae are..." I pause, trying to figure out the best way to tell Jade just how careful she needs to be without freaking her out more. She grew up in a town without fae residents, and until coming to Thunderbird Academy, never even met one. But it wouldn't be smart to lie to her, so I settle on the truth. "Fae are dangerous. They're cunning, and they are not your friends. If the queen put these rules in place, she is doing us a kindness very uncharacteristic of her kind. They also cannot lie, and that means, as long as we follow the rules, we'll be safe."

"You make them sound like villains."

"Because they are."

Jade stares at me in shock, as if not quite believing my words. I stand, moving from one side of the room to the other, feeling restless.

"Don't you for a second think these creatures are on your side. They only look out for themselves."

"But I don't understand. You have a fae friend. There are others here..."

"They're different. We're at the queen's mercy now. She is not our friend."

"Follow the rules, Jade." I point to the piece of paper she's holding in her hands. "Stay away from strangers. Don't make any bargains or promises or wishes."

My words settle over us, and we pause at the reality of what our lives have become. We're in a completely different situation here. And as much as I know about the fae, or even the Ancients, so many students here don't have that same knowledge. Much of this comes from how segregated the magical community has become. My mama told me other covens have a tendency to keep to themselves. Much like Jade's family, students are raised in an environment that is very one sided. It makes me so thankful to know my family made sure I knew the ways of the world.

"I'm scared, Maddie," Jade whispers, and I move instantly to her side.

"We'll get through this," I vow, even more intent on setting this right. For a moment, I consider if I should tell Jade what I did. I'm not sure if the headmaster is planning to keep it silent, or for how long it can really stay under wraps. Both Aiden and Natalie were present when I was told to create the spell. I can't see Aiden telling anyone, but Natalie seems like the kind of person who would. Especially if it benefits her.

As Jade and I get ready to head down to breakfast, my mind drifts to the shifter. Not that he's ever far from my thoughts. I didn't exactly dream about him last night, but he was there any time I closed my eyes.

The look he gave me right before Natalie pulled him out of the room haunts me. There was emotion there I didn't expect but hoped for. Yet, now that the dust has settled, I have no idea if it's all in my head. After all, he hasn't come to see me. I'm not sure why I'm even thinking he would. Just because I've developed some unwanted feelings, doesn't mean he's going to reciprocate them. Even though I think we have a connection.

Why am I even thinking about this?

I yank my sweatshirt over my head, sending my hair into frizzy disarray. I'm such a dumb Dora, I need to get my act together before it's too late. But maybe it's already too late. I'm all kinds of twisted up over a boy. That's as unintelligent as it comes.

"You ready?" Jade's question pulls me out of my thoughts, and I turn to see her standing by the door. She gives me a questioning look, clearly reading something on my face, but I push it all down. Now is definitely not the time to have a heart-to-heart about my unnecessary emotions. We're in a place that is hazardous to our health. We are in a midst of a war. I brought us here, and I should focus on sending us back.

Everything else can wait.

"Let's do this."

4

"**M**addie!" I hear my name called the moment we step into the dining room. I turn to see Ben wave as he heads toward us. My eyes instantly search for Aiden, but he's still nowhere to be found. Ben reaches me in the next second, wrapping his arms around me and sweeping me right off my feet.

"Someone is happy to see me," I mumble into his shoulder when he puts me down.

"Sorry," he replies, rubbing the back of his head as he takes a step back. "I'm just happy you're okay. I know I just saw you yesterday, and I knew you were okay, but now you're here and you're..."

"Okay?" I interrupt his babbling, and he gives me a sheepish look. I can't resist that small smile, so I step right back into his arms, hugging him around the middle. "I'm glad you're okay too."

Ben and I have become the fastest of friends, and I'm honestly not sure if I should be weirded out by that or not. He's not like the rest of his pack, and I feel a certain kinship toward him. Which is a bit strange. It's not like I have a tendency to open up to people right away, but it's as if we're on the same wavelength.

"We're going to get some food," I say, motioning toward Jade. Ben nods, stepping aside as my friend and I head for the line.

"Why were you so worried?" I decide to ask as Jade and I pile some breakfast food onto our plates. The academy has gone a little overboard today, probably trying to soothe anyone's worries, but I'm not complaining. Breakfast food is at the top of my favorites. Ben doesn't reply right away, and I look over to see him scanning the crowds.

"Ben."

"Sorry, there have been rumors."

"What kind of rumors?"

"That you had audience with the queen yesterday. And then, no one saw you after. So, I didn't really know what to think."

Great, the ever-present gossip mill is alive and well. That's an annoying turn of events considering I would've liked for people to not know I'm seeing the queen. But there's not much I can do about that now, except try and turn the gossip a certain way. My way.

"Yes, I was with queen yesterday, but it was actually before I saw you in the hallway. One of her nephews used to go to school here and is my friend. I was with him when he was summoned."

"Oh." With that one word, Ben visibly relaxes.

"What?"

"Nothing."

"Ben." I think saying his name in my stern voice is going to be the way to go. He glances at me sheepishly before looking over my head.

"We were just worried, that's all."

"We? What are you not telling me?" I grab one of his sleeves, tugging on it until he meets my eye once more. There's a look there I can't quite place, and then, he's moving away.

"I'll see you later, okay?"

"Ben!" But he's already gone.

"What was that all about?" I ask, turning to Jade, who stayed silent during the whole exchange. We grab our plates and begin making our way to a table. Noel is already seated, so we weave in and out of the aisles before finally reaching him.

"I think it may have something to do with his alpha," Jade whispers, leaning closer once we're seated. I glance at her sharply, and then twist to see if Aiden has finally decided to make an appearance. But no. He's still nowhere to be found.

"What do you mean?" I turn back to my friend.

"Just that Ben has always been here to watch over you for him. And he said, '*we* were worried.' That implies more than one person." She shrugs, giving me a quick smile before she dives into her food. I think she's right, of course. Ben has been assigned to watch me. It's how we became friends in the first place. But I still don't understand the secrecy. I knew that, so why not just say Aiden was worried?

Forcing myself to take a bite of the hash browns in front of me, I do another scan of the dining hall. This time, my eyes land on Owen, Aiden's other right hand. He's leaning against the wall on the opposite side of the room, his face turned in our general direction. While I can't exactly see his eyes from this distance, I feel like he's watching me.

It should make me feel safer, but it just makes me feel more nervous than I already am. If Aiden is so set on having me followed, then maybe he knows something I don't. There has to be a way to talk to him, wherever he is. He can't avoid me forever. We still have training, after all.

That's it. That's where I'll talk to him.

He's always taking combat training seriously, and except for a few times, has always been present. Even when we were fighting. No matter what's going on now, he has to be there. He wouldn't leave me unprepared.

Satisfied with that, I dig into my food a little more forcefully. So much is happening in such a short time, it's difficult not to get overwhelmed. But right now, for this one little thing, at least I have a plan. And that makes me feel much better.

AFTER BREAKFAST, EVERYONE CONVERGES IN THE GRAND HALL once again. It has always fascinated me how this room never seems that big, until it fits everyone in it. Now I realize, it's just another magic trick, but what in my life isn't?

"What do you think they want now?" Noel asks, coming to stand on my left side. Jade is basically plastered to my right, with Vera a few steps away with other hawk shifters. She's been keeping her distance a bit, and I'm sure it has everything to do with the fact that her roommate turned out to be evil. I don't think she's trusting anyone right now. I catch her eye, and she gives me a small nod before turning her attention to the front of the room once more. I make a mental point to try and talk to her later. Maybe she'll feel less pressured if it's just me.

"I think they're just making sure we know the plan," I reply, studying the students around me. They all look uneasy, and I don't blame them. This is not exactly what they signed up for when they came to the academy. We were supposed to be safe here; it was supposed to be the safest place for us. But things change. I've learned that better than anyone recently.

The headmaster takes the stage, and a hush falls over the student body immediately. I feel a presence at my back, my heart skipping a beat. But when I turn, my face falls in disappointment. I try to mask it, but Owen doesn't miss a thing. He gives me a small smirk as he takes his place at my back, his eyes on the head-master. Not that I don't appreciate the silence, but it always amazes me how different Ben and Owen are. Both at Aiden's side as his seconds, but where Ben is a bit like a hyperactive puppy, Owen is a wise old dog.

I shake my head a little, dispelling the analogies. I have an inkling that shifters don't like being compared to pets. Therefore, I should keep those thoughts to myself.

The other thoughts I should keep to myself are the ones currently swimming in my mind, telling me that even though

Aiden can't be here, he's still sending his guards to watch me. Does that mean he cares, or is he being cautious because I'm the one with the story spell casting ability? I really need to talk to that shifter and soon.

"Everyone has received your list of school guidelines." The headmaster is speaking, and I force myself to focus on the words. "We understand it may seem like a vast amount of rules, but they are here to help guide you in this new situation."

I wonder if he rehearsed this or if this kind of speech comes easily to him. That's when I notice Elder Matilda lurking in the shadows behind the faculty up on stage. My eyes narrow as I try to bring her fully into focus, but she's too far and too hidden. That makes me highly suspicious. It's not like the school doesn't get an occasional visit from the elders. Why would she be staying in the shadows now?

"Your morning classes have been cancelled, but the afternoon classes are to proceed as scheduled. Those of you with training, you are still to report to your instructors. Please follow the rules, and we will keep you updated as we learn more."

Well, that told us nothing new. He dismisses us then, and the students begin filing out of the room. But my eyes are still glued to the headmaster's retreating back. He stops near Elder Matilda, and the two exchange a few words. With the noise of conversation around me, I can't even focus enough to read lips. Not that I could from this distance. But I want to know what they're saying. This is when being a shifter would be helpful.

"Ready to go?" Jade asks, and her words bring me back to reality. And then I realize something. Spinning, I push through the exiting crowd and stop right in front of Owen who hasn't moved.

"Hi, bodyguard," I greet him, smiling sweetly. "Can you use that super hearing of yours, and tell me what Elder Matilda is harping on about over there?" I nod my head in the direction of the stage, but my eyes remain on Owen. He watches me for a long moment, his intensity making me squirm, but I refuse to budge. I think we're going to stand there forever, but then I see a slight tug on his lips, which tells me I won some kind of a favor. His eyes move to focus on the stage, and I glance over my shoulder to see my friends waiting for me, confused looks on their faces.

"Elder wants an audience with the queen." Owen's low voice rumbles, and I turn my attention to him. "She's not happy being stuck here. She blames you." He glances at me briefly. "She wants favor and a safe passage out. Headmaster won't have it."

I try looking over my shoulder, but just as I do, they move farther off the stage and into the shadows. Neither looks in my direction, but I have a feeling they knew what I was doing. If we're on lockdown, it would be impossible for Elder Matilda to leave. So why is she making such a fuss? Does she know something we don't? I mean, I'm sure she knows something we don't. But this does raise a few more concerns in my mind.

"Always causing trouble, are we?" Owen's question turns my attention back to him.

"Is that a joke? Are you teasing?" I place my hand dramatically over my heart. "I didn't think this day would come!"

He shakes his head, but I have a feeling he's trying not to smile. At this moment, I realize I want him on my side like Ben is on my side. Maybe I can crack this stoic shifter and then I'll have two friends for life.

"Nothing?" I say, keeping a smile on my face. "I'll crack you eventually."

"I doubt it."

"I like a challenge," I say over my shoulder as I turn to rejoin my friends. Even that exchange was more than I've gotten from him since school began.

"What was that about?" Noel asks as I reach them.

"Just a friendly hello," I reply.

C lasses go by in a blur. I'm hardly paying attention, but I think that goes for everyone at the moment. It would be easy to forget we're not in our realm anymore, if not for all the extra fae walking around. I'm not saying they're making me nervous, but they are making me uneasy. It doesn't matter that those two things are nearly the same, one makes me sound a little braver than I feel.

"Do you have training today?" Jade asks as we head for our room after our last class. Neither one of us felt like eating lunch today, so we grabbed some fruit on our way to our side of the castle.

"I'm supposed to," I reply. "I haven't heard otherwise, so I'm assuming yes."

I try not to let the excitement I'm feeling show on my face. Well, maybe not excitement. Anticipation? I just need to see Aiden with my two eyes to make sure he's okay and then I'll go back to ignoring everything I feel for him. How's that for a plan?

"Yeah, I think your shadow would've mentioned it."

I turn to where Jade is looking and see Owen leaning on the wall by the opposite staircase, his eyes on me. He's been there all day. I haven't seen Ben at all, but Owen has followed me like the

28

shadow Jade says he is. Not that I'm complaining. I do feel safer with him around. I have conflicting emotions on the matter. Aiden should know I can handle myself. Even though I feel like I can't at the moment. But also, having Owen at my back calms me somehow.

The doubts and fears creep in suddenly, as if they were waiting their turn to populate my brain all day. I don't like this feeling. I don't like keeping things from my friends. I don't like having this power inside of me that can ruin everything with just a few words. At least while I was in class, I could pretend I was focusing on the course work. But now, I have no excuses for the thoughts rushing through my mind.

When Jade and I reach the room, we both head for our beds. It's like the day has drained us in more ways than one. Lying down, I look up at the ceiling, my thoughts drifting over to the secret library. If there is a place that has an answer for my predicament, it has to be there. But I have no way of reaching the greenhouse unnoticed. And I can't even be sure the library is there. Maybe the place is more attached to our realm than the school. Or maybe its magic is blocked here in Faery. I'm going to have to talk to Liam about it. If I see him anytime soon. I really thought he'd be joining the academy once again now that we're here, but I haven't seen him since yesterday. I can go over all the ifs and whens until I'm blue in the face, but it doesn't change the facts. I have no idea what I'm doing. Yet somehow, with the thoughts of the fae, I drift into sleep.

There's a thick fog all around me, so much so I can barely see two feet in front of me. With the fog comes the chill of an early morning, but it goes even deeper than that. I glance down at myself and find I'm not wearing my usual clothing. A deep green gown shifts around my legs, and when I move my hands over the material, I find the corset full of jewels. My shoulders are exposed, and so is a good portion of my back. The chill becomes cold as goosebumps race up and down my arms.

Doing a quick three-sixty, I realize I have no idea where I am. There are no markers for me to go off of, just fog and darkness beyond it. Reaching out with my left hand, I lift the dress up with my right. Taking tentative steps, I move forward with my hand outstretched. I haven't taken but few steps when my hand hits something. It's a tree, and that's when I realize I'm in a forest.

Once again, I study my surroundings, but there are no clues for me to find. Even after all the survival lessons, I have no defense over a forest where moss doesn't grow. I have no idea how I got here or why I'm here. Having no other choice, I start moving forward, keeping my steps as light as possible. Automatically, I reach for my battle magic, but I don't feel it. That makes me pause, a burst of panic in my chest, but I quickly push it down. It would do me no good to lose control right here and now. My mind races with the possibilities of what this means. I don't remember this dress. I don't remember getting here. I just opened my eyes, and the fog was in front of me.

That makes me pause.

I stop moving, doing another quick scan before I call on my magic. Nothing happens. That's when it comes to me.

I'm dreaming.

"I wondered how long it would take you to figure it out." The voice comes from beyond the fog, neither male nor female but some kind of distortion in between sounds. It makes me disoriented, so I put a hand out, searching for a tree I can lean against. The moment my skin touches the bark I feel more grounded.

"Who are you, and what am I doing here?"

"Learning. Growing." I don't miss the way the voice ignores my first question. My eyes narrow, as I try to see through the fog, but it's useless.

"What am I learning?"

"The way of the story."

That makes me pause, a million question come to mind. But which one to ask to actually receive an answer I can use? Before I can utter another word, the voice speaks again.

"Do not be afraid of the story. Let it flow through you, and it will be complete."

There is a rush of wind, sending my dress flying as it envelops me.

"Wait!" I call out, but somehow, I know the voice is gone. I battle the *dress into submission, but it's no use. The wind is everywhere and then I'm spinning.*

I sit up with a gasp, sweat dripping down my neck.

"Are you okay?" Jade asks, looking up from her history book. Glancing down, I see that I'm once again in my dark jeans and blue t-shirt. Reaching for my magic, I feel it dance inside me and instantly feel better.

"Yeah, just a bad dream."

"Sorry," Jade replies, genuine concern in that one word, and I try for an encouraging smile. "You better hurry though. You have training in thirty minutes. I was about to wake you up."

I glance at the clock, realizing the time. With a quick thanks, I jump off my bed and reach for my workout attire. Finally, I'm about to check one thing off my to-do list. It's time to have a conversation with Aiden.

🧿

THERE ARE FIVE MINUTES TO SPARE WHEN I ARRIVE AT THE training building. One my way over, I noticed there are hardly any students outside on the lawn. Even though the whole campus was transported to Faery, no one is spending their time by the fountain or the avenue of limes. I think we all feel a little unsure of the air around us, even though the surroundings look familiar.

For just a second, I think he won't be there. But when I open the door, I feel him even before I see him. He's standing on the opposite side by the windows, and when I step inside and shut the door, he turns slowly toward me. I don't have shifter eyesight, but even at this distance, I can feel the intensity in his gaze. There so much emotion there, so much that he usually keeps inside.

I don't know what to do with myself as I try to figure out what he's thinking. My skin goes hot under his gaze, and I keep myself from moving forward before I'm ready. Before he's ready. I'm waiting for him to speak, to do anything, in that way I've only dreamed about. But he doesn't move forward, he doesn't come to me. So, I have to be the brave one.

Tentatively, I take a step toward him as I wipe my clammy hands on my leggings. A drop of sweat runs down my spine, and I'm sure with his shifter senses he can feel the intensity coming off me like steam.

"Where would you like to start today?" I say because the only thing I can do is pretend everything is as it was. I can't think about the fact that I'm feeling all these emotions, or the fact that I am ecstatic about seeing him alive and well. Then, I'm only five feet in front of him, and I don't know if I can get through training without giving something away. We've never been friends, and after Natalie arrived, we can never be anything more. But he stood by me in battle, he had my back in the headmaster's office. That has to count for something.

I open my mouth to say something else, to ask another question, but then his arms are around me, and he's lifting me straight off the floor, and all I can do is cling to him like I never want to let go. He lifts me even higher, burying his face in my collarbone, and I twine my legs around his middle to pull him even closer. I'm not sure who's comforting whom here, but we both need this. So, I don't speak, I don't move, I just hold him as tightly as I can, with his arms wrapped around me.

After what seems like hours, we pull back at the same time. With the way he's holding me, I'm finally looking down at him, instead of the other way around. The colors in his eyes dance, changing from light to dark, similar to the storm that's brewing inside of me. Emotions rise up within me, and I try to fight the urge, but I can't seem to control myself or my emotions. Being a shifter I'm sure he can tell what I'm feeling even more so than I can. One of his arms trails down my back while the other pins me to his front. I shudder, fully aware that I'm putty in his hands, and I don't care. The electricity dances around us, and my magic is doing a rumba within me. When I lean down, he moves to match me and then we're only a breath away.

But before our lips can touch, he jerks away, placing me gently on the ground and moving to the opposite side of the room with his supernatural speed. I'm breathing heavily as I force my legs to keep me upright. The sting of rejection almost takes the breath out of my lungs, but I can't let him see just how much he's affecting me. I think I finally have a hold on myself when the door opens at my back. Twisting around, I watch Natalie step into the room.

Her eyes zero in on me, and it's like she's studying me from the inside out. She carries with her a different kind of an intensity, but after the rollercoaster of emotions I just went through, I'm not backing down. I'm tired of cowering from situations or events. Maybe if I was braver in the first place, my spell would've done its job properly.

"There you are," Natalie coos, walking farther into the room and heading straight for Aiden. He turns just in time to catch her kiss on his cheek and the burst of jealousy that springs up inside of me doesn't go unnoticed. Natalie gives me a smug smile before focusing on Aiden. "I thought we had plans."

"For later," he replies, not meeting my eye. "I have training for the next hour. I'll meet you after."

"I'll just stay and watch..."

"No."

The word is sharp, and even though I'm not a shifter, I can hear the alpha in that one word. Aiden still hasn't met my eye, and I proceed to do stretches as Natalie pouts.

"Awe, but I would love to see these hard muscles at work now. Instead of waiting until later."

I almost face plant as I drop my foot from where I was stretching it behind my back. My eyes stay glued to the floor as I move my arms over my head, but I'm sure at least Natalie is looking at me in that smug way of hers.

"I'll see you after," Aiden says, and this time, he leaves no room for arguments. Natalie does her little disappointed sigh and turns to go.

"See ya later, Maddie," she calls, finally acknowledging my existence.

"Bye," I reply, and thankfully it doesn't come out as bitter as I expect it to. She can tell I'm not exactly her fan. Being a shifter does give her a certain upper hand in these situations.

Aiden and I don't speak immediately after she leaves. I continue my warmup as he walks around the room. I have so many things I want to ask him, but once again, I have no idea who we are to each other. There are words I want to say but won't. No matter how brave I'm trying to be. But this thing with Natalie? I can't let myself forget it. He's promised to her. It's their way. Even if Aiden was into me as much as I am into him, there could never be a future for us.

"I wanted to come see you after." He speaks up, and I stand up straight, all thoughts of exercise forgotten. If this is the only conversation we get, I'll take it.

"Why didn't you?" I'm almost afraid to ask, but I need to know.

"I had to take care of my pack first." He means her, of course. She's part of his pack now. They're merging hers and his together, so Natalie is at the top of his list.

"I understand." Turning away, I reach for my water bottle because suddenly my throat is closing up, and I can't seem to stop the flood of emotions I'm feeling.

"I don't think you do."

His words are so quiet, I know I'm not meant to hear them. But I do. Spinning around, I gasp when I realize he's moved closer. There's something in his eyes I can't decipher, but the desire to reach out almost overwhelms me.

"Then explain it to me," I whisper. He stares at me, rooting me to the spot, and for just a moment, I think he'll give in. That he'll cross the line and tell me everything. But he doesn't.

"I can't."

I nod at that, taking a swig of my water to push the tears down. Maybe it's the aftereffects of the magic, maybe this is what Liam feared. I'm too unbalanced. The magic inside of me is bursting to be set free in a completely new way. I can't tell if it's reacting to Aiden or my emotions or something else. But I'm fighting for control on too many fronts. I don't know if I can win.

"Thank you for sending Ben and Owen to watch out for me."

"Always."

His eyes flash with that one word and my heart thuds in my chest. Words are on the tip of my tongue, but before I can decide if I'll utter them, Aiden attacks.

❦ 6 ❧

There is no mercy in the way he moves. But after all this time training with him, I anticipate his moves a lot more than I thought I would. He's pushing me to react, and so that's what I do. When he comes at me from the side, I drop to a squat before I roll out of the way. My body has become acquainted with the physical aspect of combat and is reacting almost automatically. I'm on my feet in a flash, and when Aiden's punch comes, I block it with my arm. We dance around each other, him punching and me blocking. His knee comes up, but I bat it down. Sweat begins to drip down my skin, but he needs this as much as I do. I can see it in his eyes. They're almost all wolf, and when I meet his gaze, my own magic flares up.

When the next attack comes, it's much stronger. But so am I. I don't hesitate to infuse my thrusts with magic, giving myself the same power up Aiden receives from his wolf. We're evenly matched in so many ways. I didn't even realize how much I've learned, until this moment.

But my thoughts are a distraction because the next thing I know I'm being tackled. I land hard on my back, with Aiden right on top of me.

The feel of him on top of me is the purest sort of torture. I freeze, afraid to breathe too loudly and distort the serenity I feel with him next to me. He pushes himself onto his elbows, glancing down at me as if he too wants this moment to last a little longer.

Neither one of us understands it, but here we are.

The intensity in his gaze is more than I can take, but still, I don't move. Maybe I'm being a coward, but I don't want to be the one to put a name to whatever is happening here. I don't want to be disappointed when it's not the word I would use.

Aiden's eyes land on my lips before he brings them back up to meet my eyes. My heart stops beating and then restarts with a ferociousness I don't expect. The shifter doesn't miss a thing, and his eyes are all wolf as he looks down at me. One of us is going to break, and I'm afraid it might be me. It's the fear that drives me and then I'm pushing him off me as we roll. He catches on quickly, but not quickly enough, which gives me time to escape.

"I count that as a win," he comments, getting to his feet. My face feels flushed, and I hope it's only red from exertion.

"I don't," I reply before I attack.

There's something freeing in the way we spar. I've never would've imagined myself as someone who loves combat training, yet here we are. Of course, I wish to never have to use it, but I know better than to expect that from my life. It hasn't exactly been all cupcakes and unicorns. Although that last part is probably a good thing since unicorns are vicious.

"You're not focused," Aiden calls out, and I glare at him.

"I'm focused."

"Not enough."

"Oh yeah? And how do you know?"

"Because I know you."

Those words burrow into me and take residence deep inside. Maybe I'm foolish to take these small glimpses of his character, but I can't help myself. When he says things like that, it's like he's talking to my very soul. There's no arrogance, no distance between us. It's a genuine truth, and I hold onto it. Doesn't everyone want to be known, truly known? But I can't let him see how those words affect me.

"Maybe you don't know as much as you think," I reply with a grin and then I throw myself at him. He turns, but as my body connects, I use the momentum to send us tumbling as I wrap my arms and legs around him. We roll a few times, but I don't let go. My arm is wrapped tight around his neck, and my legs are criss-crossed over his stomach. I hold on as he struggles, but he taught me well. Unless he goes full wolf, he's not getting out of this one. When he taps me on the hand, I release, and he tumbles out of my arms and next to me.

We lay side by side, both of us breathing heavily.

"You're getting better."

"I know."

For some reason, both of us find that funny. I laugh, and he chuckles, and this moment is going into my memory box. Because no matter how much we are not meant to be together, he's always going to have a place in my heart.

As I make my way toward the castle, my body breaks out in nervous sweat. It's not that I've never dealt with the fae before. But this is different. This is the High Queen of Spring Court. She is ruthless and cunning, and she thrives on power. I can't pretend to be brave around her. I have to actually have the courage.

When I'm only halfway across the school grounds, Liam steps out of the trees. I pause, surprised to see him, but I really shouldn't be. He said he'd come see me when he had the chance. And no matter how I feel about the rest of his people, I know he has my back. My two seconds of doubt are not earned. He's never done anything but stay by my side.

"Are you here to escort me to the queen?" I ask as he comes up to stand in front of me.

"I'm here to make sure you're safe," he replies. His quiet words soothe my worries because I know he'll stand by them.

"Did you think I wouldn't be?" I ask, genuinely curious.

"You know better than to assume anything otherwise."

And that's the truth of Faery. No one is safe while we're here. I told this to Jade, and I wasn't exaggerating. He gives me a quick once over, as if making sure everything is as it should be and then turns to fall into step beside me. There's a moment of silence, but then I ask what's bugging me.

"What are you so worried about?"

At first, it seems like he's not going to reply. The fae have to be careful with how much they say, and what kind of questions they answer, because words have power here. I'm not so naive to think Liam has given me his true name. I don't know if anyone knows that. But he has shared more with me than he's shared with probably most people.

When we first met, it was instant kinship. At the time, I was too nervous to question it. I needed a friend, and he was there. But it was easy to be around him, and after I learned more about his kind, I wondered if he did something to make me like him. After the Ancients started their attacks and I became surer of myself and my magic, I asked him about it. He told me he never had to use his glamour to make me like him. He felt connected to me in a way he didn't expect. So, he stuck around to see where it would lead. It led to us finding that secret library and forming a friendship that is odd to a lot of supernatural beings.

That's not to say that fae are unfriendly bunch. Actually, no, they are unfriendly. They keep to their own people. Sure, quite a few cross the boundaries when it comes to shifters, since shifters have some of the same glamour magic running in their veins. And they're just as promiscuous as the fae. But it's never been like that between us and right now, I'm beyond thankful. Especially since everything else is weird in my life, including Aiden, and I need the stability I find in our friendship.

"I don't like her fascination with you," Liam finally replies, and

I don't have to ask who *her* is. I'm not exactly thrilled by her attention either, but it's not like I can do much about that. I did kind of drop a whole school into her forest.

"It'll be fine. I know what to expect."

"I don't think you do."

That makes me pause. I stop moving and wait for Liam to explain. He stops but doesn't turn around, as if his mind is lost somewhere else.

"Liam, talk to me."

I need to know what I'm walking into. He seems to have some kind of knowledge he thinks I don't. Having no other choice, I wait him out. This is definitely a skill I developed a little more fully after dealing with Aiden. Silence doesn't have to be filled for it to be powerful. People have a tendency to get unconformable when there's too much of it. Not that I think Liam will fall for that. But he knows what I'm doing, and that's what finally gets to him.

"I told you this when you arrived, you need to be careful with your magic. I don't want you to get hurt. And she," he pauses for a moment before carrying on, "she won't hesitate to have you hurt if it works in her favor. Just remember that when she begins promising you great things."

"She's just as nervous as we are," I say, and Liam's eyes fly up to meet mine. "The Ancients are after all of us. I've never thought anyone on this planet would be as old as the fae, but the Ancients are here now. And they're at the border of Faery. You think she'll promise me great things because she needs me. But that means she can't do this on her own."

"Don't do that, Maddie." Liam moves forward, placing gentle hands on my shoulders. "Don't try to rationalize her behavior or motives. Be smart and always on your guard. That's how you survive."

We stand like that for a long moment, me looking up at him, his hands on my shoulders. There's an understanding that flows between us, and I realize I've missed that. A pure kind of emotion not clouded by anything else.

"Look who it is." A voice sounds from our left, and Liam and I turn as one to watch Natalie step out of the shadows. My heart leaps into my throat when I see Aiden right behind her. His eyes are on me, fire sending the color into disarray.

"I'm Natalie," the shifter announces, looking Liam up and down. The fae has dropped his hands from my shoulders, but he's moved to stand close enough that his arm grazes my own. "I don't think we've had the pleasure."

My magic flares up at her sweet tone, and Liam's hand moves to capture mine. The contact calms me, but then a growl swings my eyes to Aiden once more. His are entirely focused on where Liam's hand holds my own, and I can see the wolf emerging. Instinctively, I release Liam's hand, but he won't let go. I glance at him and find his hard gaze on Aiden. The two are now in a full stare down, and I'm afraid to see this go any further.

"This is Liam," I say, trying to diffuse the situation with my voice. Aiden's eyes shift to mine, and I almost stumble under the heaviness I find displayed there. "This is Natalie and Aiden."

"Shifter," Liam nods a greeting.

"Fae," Aiden replies, his words full of ferocity. His wolf is close to the surface and a part of me wants to step forward and reach for it. My fingertips long to be buried in Aiden's silky fur, and I curl my free hand into a fist by my side to control the desire.

"It's a pleasure," Natalie says, and it sounds anything but. She doesn't miss the way Aiden is reacting, if the hatred she's throwing at me is any indication. "We should be going."

She wraps her arm around Aiden's turning him in the direction of the school. At first, I don't think he's going to move, but then, as if resigned, he does. Natalie throws another hard glare my way and then they're walking away. I watch their retreat, perplexed by what just happened. One minute, Aiden doesn't want anything to do with me, the next he's ready to get into a battle with a fae. How am I supposed to figure him out?

"So, that's interesting."

Glancing at Liam, I squint at him in question. He gives me a small smirk before pulling me toward the castle, since he's still holding my hand.

"What was that?" I reply, tugging my hand back. This time, he lets go.

"Nothing."

"That wasn't nothing." It's my turn to glare, which earns me one of Liam's rare chuckles.

"No." I grab his sleeve, pulling him to a stop. This is a move I wouldn't try with anyone else but him. "Tell me."

"You've become very demanding, you know that?"

"Yes. Because I deserve to be treated fairly." I place my hands on my hips, trying to make myself appear taller. Liam grins, not missing what I'm trying to do.

"I like this side of you."

"Goodie. Now can you tell me why you were acting like a Neanderthal?"

"Because shifters are fun to mess with."

He takes off toward the castle then, not bothering to explain. I hurry to catch up, burning questions on the tip of my tongue. But then, I see the guards at the front gates, and the questions die on my lips. I have more pressing issues to focus on right now than boys being boys. I'm about to see the queen.

7

L iam leads me through the hallways in silence. I'm thankful for his presence, but I'm still nervous. There's no going around that. When we reach the massive carved doors, two guards standing on each side, Liam pauses.

"Aren't you going in?" I ask, glancing behind me.

"This is where I leave you," he replies.

"Oh," is all I can manage, but that's all Liam needs to hear. Stepping forward, he reaches for my hand, giving it a quick squeeze.

"You'll be alright. Just be smart and careful," he whispers just as the guards move to open the door. That's my cue. Quickly, before I lose my nerve, I head for the entrance. The moment I step inside, the doors are shut at my back, and I'm alone.

The room is large, shaped similarly to the secret library, with a big open space and a large dome ceiling in the middle. The one big different I notice immediately is all the drawings. Every part of the dome is covered in paintings depicting the fae world. There are beautiful women in gorgeous dresses, handsome men in their fine coats. There are battles and bloodshed, as well as romance and dancing.

"Beautiful, is it not?" The queen speaks, stepping out of the shadows at the opposite side of the room. I had no idea she was already in here, and it freezes me for a second. Then, I remember myself and curtsy, hoping my little lapse of decorum isn't too noticeable.

"It is. Does it tell a story?"

"It does." The queen continues to make her way toward me slowly, as if she's circling her prey. Which truth be told, that's exactly what I feel like I am. "It is the history of the court and the battles we fought against one of our greatest enemies."

I'm too afraid to ask what enemy that could be. Outside of the Ancients, the fae are the most powerful beings within the realms. I can't image what could be more powerful.

"Come, child." The queen motions me forward as she lowers herself onto a window seat. Tentatively, I walk toward her, taking the seat opposite. With Liam's warnings and my own misgivings, I have no idea how to act or what to say. The queen continues to study me, and I almost ask her what she sees.

In the past few months, I have changed in more ways than one. I discovered more about my magic, and I've had to be stronger about standing on my own. But I've also been in combat training while spending restless nights researching. All those things take a toll on the body, one way or another.

"You are afraid." The queen finally speaks up, breaking the silence. I'm so surprised by the sound, I don't contradict her. Maybe I should. Maybe I should play at being braver than I feel. But I have a feeling she would be able to tell.

"This whole situation is scary." I settle on the truth, without being direct about it. She surprises me by laughing, the sound melodic and hypnotizing as it rings out around us.

"You are a smart girl, Madison Hawthorne. You know the ways of the words."

For some reason, her statement brings a pang to my chest. Maybe it's the memory of my father saying something similar when we were creating one of our slang lists. He always made sure I understood the words I was researching, and so we would construct difficult sentences to help me. Now, it seems that's paying off in more ways than one. His memory emboldens me to utter my next question.

"If I may, Your Highness, why am I here?"

The queen doesn't answer immediately, sending those calculating eyes to study my face thoroughly. It's not my place to question someone of her stature, but I can't keep making up scenarios in my mind. None of them end well.

"I am fascinated by you, little witch," she finally replies, and I can't quite get a read on her tone. Everything she says sends chills up my back. "Your magic has broken through our boundaries and yet, you have no idea how it was done. You do not know your own power, and that is the most fascinating aspect of all."

"You want to...study me?"

That laugh rings out again, sending unpleasant goosebumps to my arms. It's difficult, but I keep myself from fidgeting. At least I can keep the outward appearance of maturity.

"I want to discover more of your power." So, she can use it. She doesn't have to say it; I'm smart enough to figure that part out. But maybe this can go both ways. The fae have been around long enough that they would have information others may not. After all, there was a reason why Liam's brother came to my hometown. He brought some very important pieces of history with him that helped us find a way to battle the Ancients and their minions.

Now I'm in a perfect position to gain more knowledge. I just have no idea how to go about it, besides agreeing to whatever the queen proposes.

"What are you proposing?" I ask before I lose all the nerve.

"You are required to practice your magic, are you not?"

"Yes."

"My proposition is that you do it here, within these walls, with me as your teacher."

"You want to teach me to use my magic?" I'm not exactly sure how that's supposed to work. Fae magic and witch magic are not the same. We follow different rules, we practice it in our own ways. The only similarities we have is our connection to nature.

"I can teach you how to use a type of magic. There are ancient practices that can benefit both sides of the power. While I teach you, you learn more about yourself. We can help each other."

She makes it sound so reasonable, as if this is the easiest decision to make. Why wouldn't I want to learn more about my magic? But I also know this is a bargain in the making, and that is not something I'm prepared to get into. Any bargain with the fae, however small, can result in imprisonment or death. And I'm already imprisoned in this realm. Yet, I also understand I can't refuse her. Doing so can end with me in the exact same position, except minus the knowledge I can glean from her. I really wish I could talk to my sisters and my parents. I could use their guidance right about now.

But then suddenly, I think about Aiden. How he's bound by duty to marry an alpha from another pack. How he's sacrificed part of his happiness to do what is right for his people. Isn't that what I would be doing? Is my staying in Faery so bad if I save my family and my friends?

"I can see you have much knowledge of our ways, Madison Hawthorne." The queen's voice penetrates my thoughts. "I will give you until tomorrow to decide. Then, a decision will be made for you."

She's playing at being nice, we both know that. But I take what I can get. I stand, knowing my next stop is to see the headmaster. Maybe he'll be able to help me make the right decision. Or come up with an alternate plane. I curtsy again before speaking.

"Until tomorrow."

WHEN I STEP OUT OF THE ROOM, MY MIND IS WORKING A MILE A minute. There are so many possibilities here, so many ways being Faery can be the worst thing that has happened to us. Up until this moment, I didn't want to admit to myself just how bad it all can be. Yes, I told Jade to be careful. I listened to Liam's warnings. But sitting in that room with the queen of the Spring Court, it has made me feel powerless. Even with all my magic, I'm nothing compared to her or what she can do to me if she puts her mind to it. And none of my friends is safe. I really screwed up.

So lost in my thoughts am I that when I finally do look up, I'm in a part of the castle I haven't seen. Everything is just as beautifully blinding as the room I left but somehow even more intimidating. The plant carvings that adorned the door spread across the walls here. When I look closely, they look like vines with leaves and flowers growing out of them, but they're gold. When I touch them, the metal is cool under my fingertips. Even so, the plant seems to be moving and breathing somehow, as if it's alive. I jerk my hand away and proceed to walk farther.

Most of the doors are shut, but there are a few open ones. Even though I'm so curious to go inside, I'm not about to diverge from the main hall. I don't want to get so lost that I can't get out. When voices reach my ears, I breathe a little easier. Maybe I can be pointed the right direction.

But when I reach the open doorway, I stop in my tracks. A group of noble fae sit around the room. Their clothes sparkle with each move they make, some in more elaborate outfits than others, but they all look like magic. They're laughing at something in the middle of the room while drinks are being passed around. The glee is so tangible, I can almost taste it from where I'm standing. Moving a little closer, I try to see the cause of their enjoyment. One of the noble fae moves and then my eyes land in the middle of the room.

A boy, not much older than myself, is at the feet of one of the fae women. He's barely dressed, just a pair of shorts, but his chest is tanned and magnificent. He clearly takes care of himself. But right now, he doesn't look like he's doing so. He's massaging one of the women's feet as she pokes him across his body with her other. However, he's not fazed. One of the others speaks up, and the moves swiftly to begin massaging them across their whole body. At first, I'm confused at why he's being pulled in all directions like a puppet. But then he turns, and I see there's nothing in his eyes but a vacant faraway look.

Instantly, my blood grows cold. They've glamoured him into servitude. I can see it now, as plain as day. Even if I tried going to him, he would reject my offer of help. He's a puppet, and they're enjoying themselves tremendously. Disgust and fear battle for the top place in my emotions, and I think I'm going to be sick to my stomach.

Turning, I race blindly for an exit. I'm not even looking where I'm going. All I can see is the empty face of the human boy as he parades around the fae, servicing them in every way possible. I'm not so naive to think they stop at him fetching drinks or doing measly massages. The fae's cruelty has never been more evident than in this moment, and I brought us here.

Gasping for breath, I stop running and look around my surroundings. I have no idea where I am. The disgust diminishes as the fear takes over. I'm full on panicking now, because if I'm lost in these halls, I may never find my way out again. My father always said if I'm lost in the forest, the best thing I can do is sit in one spot and wait to be found. It does no one any good if I'm wandering aimlessly while waiting to be found. But who's going to find me here? Maybe Liam will eventually come looking for me, but I'm not even sure about that. He has no reason to think I'm lost in the castle when all I was supposed to do is walk in and out of the meeting with the queen.

But it's still my best option. So, I find a spot against the wall where the gold vines don't go as far down and sit. If I had my phone, I could call Liam to come get me. There are so many aspects of this situation that are my fault, I don't care what anyone else says. I can't stop feeling guilty or scared. I guess I'm not that brave after all. The pretense was bound to fail me eventually.

I'm not sure how long I sit in the hallway before I hear someone coming toward me. Refusing to be found wallowing on the floor, I stand, ready for whoever it is. Then, a figure steps forward, and I forget all pretense. I throw myself at him, and he catches me easily. His arms wrap around me as if they're made to do so. He holds me closer than close, my body molding into his, and I feel one hundred percent safe.

"What are you doing here?" I mumble against his chest. I don't care how pathetic I look right now, I need this.

"I felt your fear."

That breaks through my little cocoon of happiness, and I take a step back.

"You might want to explain that to me, Aiden."

8

"There's nothing to explain," the shifter replies, putting a good three feet of distance between us. It's as if we've forgotten to be enemies. This is the second time in two days he's offered me comfort. And I returned the favor.

"Aiden."

"Come on, Duchess. We need to get out of here."

He doesn't wait for a response but turns and walks back the way he came. Seeing no other choice, I hurry to catch up. I open my mouth to ask more questions but one look at his face, and I close it back up. He's concentrating, his senses attuned to our surroundings. With his shifter hearing, he probably hears way more than I would want to, so I stay quiet.

After what seems like hours, we find ourselves outside. I haven't seen this part of the castle, and after a quick study, I realize we're in a garden. The trees are planted in little circles, and there are a few sitting areas and two fountains from what I can see. It's not a large place because from where we're standing, I can see the wall surrounding the area on all sides.

"Aiden?" His name is all I can manage because I have no idea how we're getting out. At least we're not inside anymore. The castle was truly becoming suffocating. The shifter doesn't reply but leads the way to the opposite side of the garden, stopping at the wall.

"Do you trust me?"

The question comes out of nowhere, and while I understand the context, it feels more heavily weighted than in just this moment. But for some reason, I don't hesitate.

"Yes."

There's a sharp intake of breath on Aiden's part, as if he didn't quite expect that answer. I swear his eyes grow more intense, and now I feel unsure of my footing. My body is responding on its own, and I don't think I'll ever understand it. All I want to do is pull him close and never let go. When he does take a step forward, it's my turn to catch my breath.

"I'm going to have to touch you. May I?" He hasn't asked before, but I guess in training, it's just part of what we do. This feels much more intimate. I nod, seeing no other choice, and he steps up close enough that our bodies are flush together. His arms circle my back before he sweeps me right off my feet. I yelp, just a little, wrapping my arms around his neck.

"What are you doing?" My voice comes out breathless, as he holds me like I weigh nothing.

"Getting you out of here."

Then, before either one of us can say anything else, he squats and jumps. I feel the wind on my cheeks and clothes for just a moment before we land on the other side of the wall. Amazed at his power, I can't seem to look away. I knew shifters had some of their animal abilities while in their human form, but I've never seen them demonstrated so blatantly. Now that I think about it, shifters have a tendency to keep those powers a little bit of a secret.

But he let me see it. It feels even more intimate than the fact that he's still holding me in his arms. Something passes between us, something different and new, and I know he feels it as his eyes grow darker. My pulse jumps, and I can't hide it. Not when I'm this close to him. One of us has to break this moment, or we'll stay lost in it forever.

"Thank you," I push past my dry lips, and the sound is enough to bring us back to the present. He sets me down gently, taking particular care to make sure I'm firmly on the ground before he takes a step back.

"You're welcome."

That's all I get before he steps around me and begins making his way deeper into the forest. The forest we're not supposed to go in. Not done with this conversation, and refusing to be left alone, I follow.

"What did you mean you felt my fear?" I ask, not about to let go of that particular piece of information. There are too many unanswered questions in my mind right now. I don't need to add any more to that list.

"Drop it, Duchess."

"You know I won't."

He growls then, which brings a grin to my lips. It's like he brings out the fighter in me. For some reason, when I'm around him, all I want to do is get a reaction from him. He's too unreadable for me to do anything else.

"I could just start making scenarios up on my mind," I continue, smiling sweetly even though he's walking in front of me. "Or I could just bug you until you tell me. Tell me. Aiden. Tell me."

"Are you planning on stopping anytime soon?" Aiden asks, twisting around and making me halt in my steps before I run into him. He narrows his eyes, but I like seeing him riled up. It means he's not as immune to me as he pretends to be.

"I'm not planning on stopping at all. You should just tell me." He grunts again, rolling his eyes before he turns and continues walking. I glance around then, realizing we're much farther from the academy than I thought. I don't see it through the trees anymore. Not that I'm nervous. Shifters have an impeccable sense of direction. Even in places they've never been before.

"Aiden."

"You're annoying."

"Right back at ya, Mrs. Grundy."

That makes him stop. He turns, this time a little slow, and gives me a confused look.

"What does that even mean?"

I have to think for a second which part he'd be confused about. I'm so used to using these terms, I don't even think about them.

"Mrs. Grundy is an oldies slang for an uptight individual," I explain, raising my eyebrows a little. He shakes his head at me before a quick smile blossoms onto his face. It's there, then it's gone so quick, I almost miss it.

"You and your slang."

"You and your avoidance tactics." I'm grinning up at him, and I think he's actually fighting the urge to answer in kind. We've been so off about each other, I'm not sure how to act around him anymore. This exchange is not helping.

"Ever since the dance," he begins, surprising me into silence. "I can tell when you're in danger."

I HAVE NO IDEA WHAT TO SAY TO THAT. FOR WEEKS NOW, I thought what I've been feeling, this awareness toward Aiden, was completely one-sided. But it's not. He just reacts to it in a different manner.

"Is it just when I'm scared?" I'm almost afraid to ask, but I need to know. If he can decipher my emotions without me knowing it, that would get real awkward, real fast.

"I think it's mostly when you're in so much a distress, it's a physical danger to you."

His words make me want to deny my fear, but if he can feel it, what's the use? But that actually makes me pause for a moment.

"Is this why you've been more standoffish around me?" How I'm asking all these direct questions is beyond me. But I'm not backing down. That much I know. Waiting for him to respond is a new kind of torture, that's for sure. It seems I'm still only reacting to him.

"I'm not being standoffish," he finally says before turning on his heels and beginning to walk.

"Yes, this is definitely the behavior of someone who's not avoiding anything," I mumble to his back, but of course he hears me. Stupid supernatural hearing. He spins and is in my face in a second. The intensity is physically manifested in the way his body is giving off heat. Because we're only inches apart, I feel myself grow hot from it. Or maybe it's something else. I'm too confused to try and figure out where my emotions end and his begin.

"What is it you want from me?" Aiden asks, his breath dancing over my flushed cheeks. Involuntarily, my eyes drop to his lips for a mere half second, but it's enough. His sharp intake of breath tells me he doesn't miss a thing. When my eyes meet his, the fire there nearly brings me to my knees.

"I want us to stop fighting," I answer truthfully, falling deeper and deeper into his eyes. "I want us to work together. You can help me figure this whole mess out."

With every word I say, he seems to move closer and closer. There wasn't much distance to begin with, and now our bodies are separated by a breath.

"I can't do this alone," I whisper, not caring that my heart is in my throat. "I want us to be friends."

The moment I say those words, a shudder comes over Aiden's eyes, and he takes a step back.

"I told you before, we could never be friends." He starts to move away, but I'm not done. I'm tired of this back and forth, and I need him to talk to me. So, I do the one thing you don't do to a shifter. I grab his arm, pulling him to face me. He growls, his wolf clearly unhappy with being manhandled, but he's doing the same thing to me. Expect without actually touching me.

"I thought you were smarter than this." Aiden's voice is dripping with warning, but I don't remove my hand. He feels hotter than I imagined, but it doesn't matter.

"I'm smart enough to know you answer in half-truths and even smaller sentences. Why is it so hard for you to be my friend?" A note of desperation enters my voice then, and it's too late to push back. His eyes soften, and I see the boy who held me in that shed and the one who was glad I was safe.

"I have a duty to my people, Maddie," he says, keeping his voice low. "There are things required of me that others may not understand, sacrifices I must make." For some reason, I know he's talking about Natalie and their betrothal. It's a sacrifice a seventeen-year-old should not be thinking about, yet, he doesn't have a choice.

"Because," he starts again, and a hint of emotion enters his voice making me hold my breath in anticipation. "Because being friends with you will break me, and I cannot lead my people or win this war if I am not whole."

This time, when he turns to go, I let him. Tears spring up to my eyes, and I desperately try to push them back. Every time I think Aiden and I are together, a new wall is broken down and three more are built up. We will never be anything but what we are now, but it doesn't stop every part of my being from yearning for it to be otherwise. How I have fallen so hard for someone I can never have? It's so tragic of me.

I wish I could talk to my dad. Maybe this is not something most teenagers go to their parents with, but I know my dad would say exactly what I need to hear. Being in Faery, so far away from my family, I just hope they will find some kind of lead, and the next time I'm home, my dad will be too. I spent months trying to find him, and now I'm further away from my goal than I've ever been.

Aiden slows down a little, and I realize I have fallen too far behind. Hurrying, I catch up to the shifter, but I don't speak, and he doesn't turn to look at me. We're back to our corners for now. I need to squish every emotion I have toward him and focus on the problem at hand. He can't deny me that. Not when he's trying to keep his pack safe.

"I need your help," I say, and he turns to glance at me. "I need to get to the library and see if there are any answers about our predicament. Can you get me there?"

Just like that, we're back to business. He watches me for a tense moment before he nods.

"Good. Then let's go."

9

"Is this where you've been?" I dare to ask after a few minutes of silence. The forest around us grows darker and heavier by the minute, and while I'm not scared, I would be if I was alone.

"Sometimes," Aiden replies without turning around. "I'm not exactly a big fan of the way of the fae, so I need an exit strategy, if the time comes for that."

That seems like a lot more information than he usually shares, but I'm not going to point that out. If he feels like he can talk to me, I'm going to take it and run with it. There are parts of him that are a complete mystery, even after all the time we've spent together. Maybe that's why I bring up Liam.

"Not all fae are bad."

"You mean like your little friend?" This time Aiden does look at me, but I still can't read what's going on with him. There's definitely history there, but I can't even begin to guess at it.

"Pretty sure Liam is taller than you," I point out automatically before I realize maybe this isn't the time for jokes. He'll shut down again, and I don't want him to. But Aiden surprises me once again. A small laugh escapes him before he replies.

"Yes, fae have a tendency to be giants. Got to have something going for them, I guess."

My nose wrinkles at his statement, but I don't actually hear any hostility in it. I think he might be teasing. When he steals a glance my way, I smile.

"You're hilarious."

"Oh, I know."

While the lightheartedness of the situation doesn't go unnoticed, I still want answers. So, I decide to push.

"Are you going to tell me about your feud with the fae or am I making stuff up again?"

My question makes him pause, and he turns toward me before replying.

"They're not nice creatures."

"This is coming from Mr. Friendly?" While I said the same thing to Jade, my defensive side still comes out apparently. But Aiden doesn't take the bait.

"You know I'm right, even though you're friends with one of them. You're more cautious than not."

"So, what you're saying is that you had personal experience with their...meanness, and thus refuse to give any of them a chance." It's not a question because I know I hit the nail on the head on this one. Aiden gives me one of his intense looks, narrowing his eyes slightly, before he takes a step toward me.

"You are a smart witch, Maddie. Don't let their glamour fool you."

When he says my name like that, it becomes very difficult to keep my hands to myself. It's like it requires a physical response. Instead of doing something stupid, I clench my fists at my sides.

"You're not stupid either, Aiden," I reply, needing him to understand that not everyone is cut from the same cloth. "I wouldn't think past history would keep you from future possibilities."

We're in the midst of a stare down, once again lost in a battle of wills. While I've never been confrontational before, Aiden has a way of getting under my skin. I have a slight inkling that I do the same for him. Although, shifters are already pretty confrontational. We can stand here forever because neither one of us is backing down.

Then, he does something that completely throws me off balance. He breaks eye contact for a moment before coming back and nodding.

"You're right."

"I'm sorry, what was that?" I cock my head in his direction and am rewarded by a smile for my efforts.

"I said you're right," he repeats, this time with a curl to his lips. "I wouldn't be a very smart alpha if I wasn't open to possibilities. But that doesn't mean I have to like it."

"It's a start. Once you realize I'm often right, you'll be even better."

This time, I'm the one who pushes past him and continues walking. It may not seem like a big thing, but it feels like a breakthrough. Every conversation I have with Aiden feels like that. He's a tough nut to crack, but I'm getting to him, and I'm not sure if I should be happy or nervous about that. It's not like we have a future together. Sure, one day our history may bring us an alliance. But that's all we'll ever be to each other. That thought brings genuine sadness to my heart, and I can't shake it off.

"Hey," Aiden's hand reaches for my own, a barely-there graze of his fingers on my skin sets my body on fire. He retracts his touch but not before it becomes an imprint. "Are you okay?"

Of course he can tell my emotions are changing. Not that I think shifters can read the way some witches can, but they rely on their intuition for a reason. So, instead of saying I'm fine, I give him a piece of the truth.

"I'm just worried. About everything. About how I'm supposed to fix this when I have nothing on my side to help me."

"You have me."

The statement is spoken so softly, I don't think he meant to say it out loud. But he does, and it sends my emotions on another crazy rollercoaster ride. There will never be a time when I'm around Aiden and I feel nothing. I know that now, just like I know the sun comes up in the morning and goes down in the evening. But I force myself not to react. Maybe it'll be better for both of us if I pretend I didn't hear it. Even though everything in me yearns for me to go to him and hold him until everything in my world is right again.

Something that can never be a possibility.

"Maybe the library can help. Maybe I will suddenly understand this story spell casting. I just don't want to fail everyone."

Aiden catches up to me then, stopping right in front of me so I'm forced to look up into his handsome face.

"This whole thing, it's not your fault. A responsibility was put on your shoulders in a way that no one should have to carry. No matter how bleak things may seem, you did save us. We weren't going to win, and many lives were going to be lost. But you pulled us out, and while it wasn't what we expected, we're here now. We'll make the best of it."

This, this right here is why I can never imagine him not being part of my heart. We might fight, and we might be frenemies most of the time, but he always says the right thing when I need to hear it. Afraid that I'll say something stupid, I nod instead.

"Let's get to the library," I reply, giving him a small smile.

"Actually, we're here."

AIDEN LEADS ME THROUGH THE BUSHES TO OUR RIGHT, WEAVING in and out of the greenery. I was so focused on our talk, I didn't even notice the wall-like growth right beside us. The leaves are thicker and larger than I'm used to, but Aiden doesn't offer any caution on them being harmful to us.

"Where are we?" I ask when we finally break though. The forest looks exactly the same on this side, but when I turn, I find the wall of green at my back.

OF DESTINY AND ILLUSIONS

"At the back end of the Thunderbird Academy campus line," Aiden replies before moving forward. "If you walk far enough, you'll discover there is a wall at every side of campus."

"Did the queen put that there or was it me?"

"The Queen. I think it's to prevent anyone from exploring beyond the delegated areas."

"Not that it would stop you."

"Not that it would."

We grin at each other, and as usual, his smile makes me feel calm and excited all at the same time. He motions me to follow, and I have no reservations in doing so. I've trusted him this far, but that doesn't mean I don't have questions.

"What have you found out there?"

"Nothing that can help us, that's for sure." I can feel the frustration in his voice, even though I can't see his face. As an alpha, I'm sure it's difficult for him to not have all the answers. A huge part of me wants to ask how Natalie is fits into all this, considering I saw them step out of the forest together. But I don't think I'm ready to have that conversation.

"The forest is always shifting." Aiden continues, pulling me out of my thoughts. "Every time we explore, it seems different, and it feels different. I think the queen has spelled it to keep us in one spot."

"Imprisoned, you mean?" He flashes me a quick smirk as I don't hide my dislike for her in my tone.

"Not a fan?"

"Not even a little."

She terrifies me. I'd be stupid not to fear her. But I'm also annoyed by her demands. It's not like I planned on bringing us here. And the last part, the very small part that's trying to be braver, is also fascinated. She can teach me so much about magic. Areas that the teachers at Thunderbird Academy would never even mention. After all my studies and conversations with Liam, I know fae have a particular way with the elements. After all, they created the elemental spell my sisters and I used to put a barrier around our hometown of Hawthorne. It's the only part of this whole mess that makes me feel like I wasn't a complete failure. Even though I don't trust her, maybe I can learn something from her. Isn't that the most adult outlook ever? My parents would be proud.

Just like that, my mind is on my family as I trail after Aiden. I can see sunlight on the other side of the trees and know we're getting close to the actual academy. But now I'm sad because even though I'm on campus, I'm a whole world away from my parents and sisters. Well, technically, I have no idea where my father is, so there's that. Inhaling deeply, I force my thoughts to focus on the issue at hand. Exhaling fully, my heart rate slows down just a tad, clearing my mind. It would do no one any good if I started having panic attacks now.

I notice Aiden glance at me from the corner of his eye, but he doesn't comment. He probably felt the change in me, heard the speed up of my heartbeat, but he doesn't comment. Good, I guess we're both pretending at areas in our...relationship? I don't even know what to call us. I just know what I want to call us.

"Let's run quickly," the shifter says as we come to the edge of the forest. "I don't want any wandering eyes seeing us from the building."

"If only I had supernatural speed." I chuckle, shaking out my hands as I get ready for him to say go. But instead, he turns to me with an unreadable look in his eyes. "What?"

"I can... I can carry you."

"What?"

"I run much faster than you, and if I carry you, there's a lesser chance of us being seen."

I stare at him in silence, wondering if he's being serious. When his calm and collected expression doesn't change, I realize he is.

"You didn't before, after the dance." Maybe I shouldn't be bringing that up now, but it's true. If he could've gotten us out of there sooner, why didn't he?

"I could've, but I needed to be able to fight. I wouldn't have been able to do so with you in my arms."

Every time he mentions holding me, I get a little rush of goose-bumps along my spine. Besides my curiosity on the logistics of this kind of magic, I don't want him to get in trouble. If the fae find out he's been sneaking away, it won't be taken well. And there are enough fae roaming the halls right now that any one of them could look out the window. Maybe there's always someone watching. Which is why I say,

"Okay."

I think I take both of us by surprise. But he just nods and steps toward me. His arm circles my back as I reach over to wind my arms around his neck. The proximity is doing crazy things to my heart, and that's when I realize his own is beating just as fast. He crouches for a second, sweeping my legs up with his other arm, and then I'm completely in his arms.

"Hold on tight," he whispers, his breath washing over my skin. I nod, nestling my face into the crook of his neck and then, the wind comes. I peer over his shoulder just a little and watch the forest disappear behind us in a blur.

We stop as suddenly as we began. He ran much faster than I anticipated, and I wonder if I'll ever get to experience that rush again. I'd be lying to myself if I said I didn't enjoy it. Aiden doesn't let go right away, and I have no desire to either. After a moment, I lean back, looking into his face, my arms still wrapped around his neck.

"You okay?" he asks, his voice dangerously low. Not trusting myself to speak, I nod, taking a calming breath. His scent surrounds me, and I think of rain and the forest, with a particular musk that's his alone. If it was up to me, I'd stay in his arms forever. But I know better than to wish for things, so I'm the one who moves to get down. He places me gently on the floor but doesn't move away.

"Thank you," I finally manage and then turn to look at the greenhouse. He brought us straight in, and at first, I think we're still outside. Every single plant I land my eyes on has grown tremendously. The trees are to the ceiling, all the flowers are blooming. "What's happening here?" I glance at Aiden and see that he's studying our surroundings with a type of awe as well.

"I have no idea. I haven't been in here in a while."

There's nothing I can do to stop myself from reaching for the plants. The closest to me, a type of ivy, has spread across the table and onto the floor. The leaves are plum and a gorgeous green shade, deeper than I've seen it before. I run my fingers over it gently, and my elemental magic reaches out for the plants in front of me. I feel it in the air as well as the moisture.

"It must be Faery. This realm is the strongest in their natural magics. The plants must be reacting to it." The ivy wraps itself around my hand, as if saying hello, and I smile. Nature has always been part of magical structure, but I've only seen plants react visibly a few times. Mostly in rituals class. This? This is a whole new lesson I want to learn.

Glancing up, I find Aiden has moved closer to the library's opening, and I follow him over to the crates. Without a word, we begin moving the wood away from the rug. Once that's done, I pull up the rug and yank at the door. It swings open, the stale air of the underground hitting me in the face. Without hesitation, I descend with Aiden close behind me. Liam will probably want to come visit as well, although I'm not sure how I'm going to get him in here without being seen.

When we come to the door to the library a few minutes later, something feels off. Reaching out, I place my palm against the door, and let my magic reach for the place that became like my second home. But then, a sharp pain stabs me in the palm of my hand, at the same time sending me flying from the door and straight into Aiden. He catches me easily, placing me on my feet before we both turn toward the door.

"What was that?" he asks, his hand still on my upper arm to keep me steady.

"I have no idea," I reply, the pain of rejection rushing through me. It's like the library is protecting itself against me, and I don't understand. I move forward again, and Aiden squeezes my shoulder to keep me beside him.

"What are you doing?"

"I need to know what's wrong. It's like, it's angry at me."

"It's a door, Duchess."

"Yeah, and a wand is a stick. But we both know of powerful sorcerers who can communicate with it like a friend."

Aiden has nothing to say to that because he knows I'm right.

"Just be careful," he whispers as I approach the door once more. Maybe this is what I felt when we got here, a sort of hostility coming from the library. Headmaster Marković once told me there are areas on this campus that only reveal themselves to special individuals. The library has always been my place, and only when I chose to bring others here did they find out about its existence. The library can't be mad at Aiden, he's been here before, and she's opened herself up to him with open arms. No, I think she's mad at me, and I need to know why.

"Won't you let me in?" I ask, keeping my voice gentle as I stop right in front of the door. The wood glows for half a second, before turning back into its regular brown, and I wonder what the library is trying to tell me. "Please don't be mad at me." I try again, and this time, I run one finger down the middle. I receive no response, but somehow, I know if I tried that again, I'd get hurt. Whatever is happening here, it's not something I'll be able to fix this minute.

"You've always been a friend," I whisper, pulling on my magic to make my words mean a little more. "You have helped, and you have taught. Please help me understand what's happening." I take a tiny step forward, but it's too close. The library's magic flairs up once more, sending me stumbling into Aiden.

"I don't understand." The sadness I feel is like a weight. It's like I've lost another friend, and I have no idea what to do about it.

"We'll figure it out, Maddie," Aiden says, running a comforting hand up and down my back. "All is not lost."

But now I feel more helpless than ever. This was my one chance to get an upper hand in the situation, and now it's gone. Being in Faery is messing everything up.

WE LEAVE THE LIBRARY BEHIND AND HEAD FOR THE STAIRCASE IN silence. There was so much hope riding on me being able to research and learn in that place. In the past two years, the library has become my sanctuary. Now, I can't enter it, and that's hitting me harder than I thought it would. I feel too helpless to be angry. Now, I don't know what to do.

"Do you want to talk?" Aiden finally breaks the silence when we've finished covering up the entrance and are back in the greenhouse. I must look way more lost than I feel for him to be so nice to me. But then again, he's been surprising me a lot lately. This side of him isn't as new anymore.

"Actually, I'd like to punch something," I reply before I recognize the truth to my words. Aiden grins, before motioning for me to follow. Now that we are coming out of the greenhouse, we're not as worried about people seeing us. Although, if a certain someone saw us, I'm sure there would be a lot of questions. Aiden leads the way to the corner of the building, between the academy and the greenhouse, before turning to me.

"Attack me."

"What?"

"Attack me."

"Aiden."

"You want to punch something, so do it."

"I don't want to punch you," I reply, rolling my eyes.

"Well, that seems new." He grins, breaking all my defenses. He has no idea. I sigh heavily, receiving another quick smile before he motions me forward. "Come on, Duchess. Don't tell me you're afraid of me now."

I know what he's trying to do. He's goading me into it, and I already know I'll break. The need for physical release is too loud to ignore. The past few hours have been a tsunami of emotions, and if I don't do something soon, I'll explode.

"Today would be nice."

"You really want to get your butt kicked, don't you?" Not sure where that confidence comes from, but it surprises us both. Aiden laughs, a sound I will never get tired of hearing, and I react. Pushing off my feet, I launch myself at him.

Even paying half attention, Aiden is much faster than I am. He sidesteps my attack, and I roll, getting to my feet in the same motion. Yanking the jacket off my shoulders, I toss it to the side and attack again. This time, my hands are up in front of my body, and my leg is the one that swings at Aiden. He blocks it easily, and we begin the dance.

I kick and twist, blocking and dodging most of the strikes. He's letting me lead the exercise, matching my intensity with his own. When I go to uppercut, he shoots his elbow in front of my move. My knee comes up, and he slams his palms down to block it. The move brings us closer together, so I thrust my hand up, aiming for his face. He dodges before catching my arm in his hand over our heads. Our bodies are flush together, and I try to twist out of his hold, but he yanks my arm down behind my back, bringing his other to catch me, and now I'm against his chest, with both of my arms pinned behind my own back.

"How do you get out of this?" he asks, and I'm breathing so heavily I barely hear him. I almost tell him I don't want to get out of it, but instead, I throw my knee up. He anticipates my move but doesn't move as quickly as usual, and I catch him right in the stomach. He loosens his hold on my arms just enough for me to break free, and that's when I punch him in the face. He stumbles to the side, probably more from surprise than actual pain, but now I'm fired up. I jump up to kick him in the chest, but he's already recovered. I missed my opportunity and he catches my leg, pulling it toward him. I yelp as I fly off my feet and down to my back. I land hard, the air leaving my lungs, but I'm not about to take this laying down. I kick out blindly, and then feel my foot connecting with flesh. Aiden tumbles forward, and then he's on top of me.

He catches himself on his arms, stopping just a breath above me, and we're both breathing heavily now. His eyes are doing that color changing that only comes when his wolf is close to the top.

We're both sweaty, and even though it's chilly outside, all I feel is hot all over.

"You're getting better," he whispers, his breath washing over my flushed skin.

"I've had a good teacher," I reply, without thinking. His eyes flash, dropping to my lips for a second before coming to meet my eyes once more. We're back to our standstill, knowing it can never go past this. No matter what this madness is that we're feeling. Because I'm way past pretending Aiden doesn't feel anything. It's no longer wishful thinking. It's a truth I live with now. As well as a burden I carry.

"If you use your magic when you attack, you'll be able to deliver quite a punch." He's trying to make this normal, but the fact that he's still hovering over me doesn't exactly help.

"I'll keep that in mind." I grin and then, I'm rolling out of the way. He moves his arm just in time, landing on his back before he's on his feet again. I adjust my clothing and reach for my jacket before I finally meet his eye.

"Thank you," I say, before turning to flee into the greenhouse. I may be a lot of things, but what I mostly am is a teenage girl in love with a boy I can never have. That will always be a part of me, and it's just another issue I have to deal with in my life. Because there isn't a shadow of a doubt in my mind, Aiden will stay with me for a lifetime.

❧ 11 ❧

It's been two weeks since we arrived in Faery and everything seems to have fallen into a routine. We get up every morning, we go to class, we have combat training, and we go to bed. I'm not sure what I expected when we arrived here, but it wasn't this. Everyone is acting like we aren't stuck in another realm. I'm honestly not sure how to deal with that.

On the other hand, I haven't been to see the queen since our meeting that ended with me in the woods with Aiden. She's been called away on some urgent matter, so a big part of me is just waiting for the other shoe to drop. Liam hasn't been around either, and that's making me a little concerned. Not that he owes me anything, but his disappearance isn't sitting all that well with me.

"Did you see Miss Lee's outfit today?" Jade's voice brings me back to reality and I glance up as Vera replies.

"She's wearing a very twenties dress today. Do you think she magically made it appear in her closet or she had it already?"

Thankfully, Vera has returned to our group, and things have been mostly normal between all of us. I can understand how frustrating it might be to constantly be reminded of a time you failed to see something that was right in front of your face. Okay, now I'm being extra melodramatic. It's just so ridiculous that there is nothing I can do about our predicament. I got us into this mess, and I've yet to figure out how to get us out of it. Also, the whole situation with the library is driving me insane. I've been down there two other times since that day, and both times, I ended up across the room with bruises all over my body from the impact.

"I think she had it," Noel replies before taking a huge bite of his sandwich. Since we've come to Faery, he's been training extra hard, and therefore eating a lot more. Even after a few weeks, we can all see the results. Jade, especially, is liking it. Not that they've had any sort of talk about their...relationship. I can't exactly give them any advice, since I know nothing.

Just then, I hear a few chair scrapes and look up in time to see Natalie march over to me. She pushes everyone else aside, stopping to tower over me, her hands on her hips.

"Where is he?" she nearly growls, her voice sending unwanted goosebumps over my skin.

"I have no idea who you're talking about." It's hard to appear unaffected when an alpha shifter is trying to intimidate me, but I'm holding my own. Natalie has had a bad attitude toward me since the moment she arrived. It doesn't help that she knows I was the one in the headmaster's office on the day we ended up in Faery. She hasn't spread that information around yet, but I have a feeling she would one day. Maybe today is the day.

"You know who I'm talking about. He's disappeared. Don't tell me you don't have secret meetings behind my back." Confused, I narrow my eyes at her and then I notice Ben and Owen coming up to the table. Realization hits me hard as I meet Ben's eyes.

"Aiden's missing?"

"Don't play with me, witch," Natalie nearly spits, "you know where he is."

I'm honestly baffled by the fact that she believes her own words. Standing, I'm probably not helping my situation by being confrontational, but I really don't like her towering over me.

"Why would I know where he is?" I ask, genuinely wanting to know. The question doesn't sit well with Natalie as she takes a step toward me. Then Owen is there, putting himself in her path. Ben takes his place beside me.

"Maybe we should talk somewhere else?" he says, nodding his head in the general direction of the rest of the dining room. I glance around and realize everyone's eyes are on us. Owen is close to physically removing Natalie from the room because even I can tell she's losing control. Her wolf is too close to the surface, and if she shifts in here, she won't hesitate to attack.

"Yes, let's talk somewhere more private," I say, nodding at Ben.

"Maddie?" Jade asks as she stands and places a hand on Noel's shoulder. I notice my friend has put down his sandwich and moved to spring up if he needs to.

"I'm okay, guys," I say, plastering a smile to my face. "I'm not alone." I motion to Ben and the guy gives my friends a quick smile. I know it's not ideal, but I'm not about to put my friends in the warpath of a shifter. Jade nods, but I don't miss the worry in her eyes. Owen has already led Natalie toward the outside doors, and Ben and I follow quickly.

"What is her problem?" I ask the moment the doors shut behind us and we're outside. Not that I think certain shifters can't hear us anymore, but I know most of them can't. I look over and see that Natalie has shifted and is racing toward the forest. Ben and I exchange a look and take off in the same direction. Even though Ben can shift, he doesn't, staying beside me instead. We reach the woods at the same time Owen does.

"What's happening?"

"She lost control. Give her a moment," Owen replies.

"Okay, cool. But what's happening with Aiden?"

THE BOYS DON'T ANSWER RIGHT AWAY. EVEN WITHOUT SHIFTER hearing, I can hear Natalie moving through the woods, and I have a feeling she'll be back before we know it.

"Now. I need an answer now."

Ben and Owen exchange a quick glance as I place my hands on my hips. Their caginess is making me so much more nervous. If something has actually happened to Aiden, and they're taking this long to tell me about it, there will be no stopping the wrath I unleash on these boys. I'm scaring myself a little with my thoughts, but the amount of emotions racing through me right now will get no other response.

"Ben." I level my gaze on the shifter I know best. "I know about Aiden's...recon missions. Why does Natalie think I know about his whereabouts? Where did he go?" At first, I think he's going to stay silent, but he finally concedes.

"Since you know, he's been trying to figure out why the fae are keeping us contained to the academy's grounds. We've been taking shifts, running the forest around the school, and past the hedge. Most of the time, we find nothing. Because, as strange as it sounds—"

"The forest changes." I finish his sentence, and he looks at me in surprise. Owen takes a step forward, picking up where Ben left off.

"If he told you that much, then you must know he's been looking into spell casting as well."

"What?" That makes me pause. "He hasn't said anything about that."

The shifters exchange another look, and I swear if they do that again, I'm going to scream. Going against my better judgment I step up, snapping my fingers between their faces. They jerk, swiveling their heads in my direction, and I can see they're as surprised as I am. Even though they're not alphas, they're still powerful beings, and I shouldn't be trying to rule over them in any way. Except, I can't seem to stop myself.

"Sorry, look, I..." My words leave me because I have no idea how to explain what I'm feeling or doing. It's like a tidal wave of emotions is crashing on top of me, and no matter how much I struggle to swim to the surface, I can't get my head above water.

There is an elephant sitting on my chest, making me sink farther and farther down. "What is happening to me?"

Ben reaches out, placing his hands on my upper arms as he leans over to look into my face. There's genuine concern in his eyes that pushed away any annoyance he may have had at me trying to command them into talking.

"Maddie, I think you and Aiden—"

"Ben." Owen's sharp voice cuts off whatever my friend was going to say, but I can't even lift my head to look at him.

"She must know."

"She can't. And we don't know for sure."

They continue speaking as if I'm not there, and their voices grow further away with every second. There's a dull noise filling my ears, as if I'm truly underwater. I have to get a grip on myself, or I won't be able to find Aiden. Just with that small thought, the wave crashes over me again, and I stumble to my knees. Ben follows me to the ground, still holding my shoulders, and he gives them one painful squeeze.

"Breathe, Maddie. Don't let this overwhelm you. Don't push it away. Accept it and breathe."

I don't understand his instructions. They seem to contradict each other, but I have no other choice. I'll be completely useless to Aiden if I don't pull myself together. Closing my eyes, I follow Ben's instructions, forcing the air into my lungs. At first, it doesn't seem to be working. I concentrate on the bombardment of emotions, but instead of pushing them away, I let them wash over me like rain. Suddenly, the tidal wave becomes a drizzle and my lungs open up. I gasp, taking in hungry balloons of air before I finally open my eyes.

Ben is still in front of me with Owen hovering over his shoulder. Even the stoic shifter looks concerned. But there's something else in their eyes, a secret they almost discussed in front of me. I feel exhausted, as if I actually fought through that storm.

"What was that?" I finally ask when I think my voice won't come out breathless.

"I think you had a panic attack," Ben replies before standing and helping me to my feet as well. He squeezes my hands in encouragement before letting go, and I adjust my skirt and t-shirt just for something to do. What a day to not wear jeans. It didn't feel like only a panic attack, but I don't think these boys will tell me anything. Even if I ask.

"Are you better?" This comes from Owen, and I look up to meet his eyes. Over the course of this year, I have earned at least a little bit of respect in his eyes, and for a second, I'm afraid it's gone. But it's not. Something else has joined it, and I can't decipher what.

"I am. I don't think I've ever had a panic attack before. I don't know what caused it."

"You're overwhelmed," Ben hurries to say, as if he's afraid I'll think it's something else. "So many people are putting pressure on you, and Natalie isn't helping with accusing you of Aiden's disappearance."

"Why would she think I have anything to do with it?" I still don't understand. Ben opens his mouth to speak, but then I hear a noise behind me. I turn in time to watch Natalie step out of the woods, once again in her human form.

"Because he left to help you."

12

"What do you mean he left to help me?"

I can feel panic rising from the base of my neck, but I refuse to lose control in front of Natalie. She can already smell my fear. I don't need to add any more to her fuel against me.

"Just what I said," she snaps before she gives Ben and Owen a scorching look. "You two are just as whipped as he is." She motions toward me. They don't like that; they don't like that at all. Immediately, both of them take a step in front of me, and growls like none I've heard from either of them, sounds around us. They bare their teeth, and I think they'll shift at any moment. They're ready to attack, and I have no idea why.

"Ben? Owen?" I call out, hoping my soft voice will sooth them, but they won't take their eyes off Natalie. She's glaring right back at them, as if daring them to make a move. Even though she's not their alpha, she is an alpha. She carries herself as such, and I know for a fact she carries the alpha magic in her blood. Enough of it that she can take on these two large shifters without batting an eye.

"Do not disrespect Maddie in that way again," Owen snaps, his words barely audible between his teeth. His wolf is so close to the surface, I can see it over his human form. I take a step back, afraid I'll do something to set them off, but somehow, I know they're not a danger to me. They're protecting me.

"I may not be your alpha," Natalie says, standing a little taller, her own wolf showing through, "But I will be one day, and there is nothing you can do about that. Not even if what you think is true is true."

"You know it is," Ben replies, his own growl bunching up the words. "And there's nothing you can do about that either."

Now I feel like they're talking in riddles. There has to be a way I can take control, or we'll be in this spitting match for ages, and Aiden will be out there, going through who knows what. Maybe this is foolish of me, but I do the one thing I can think of. I step up to Ben and place a hand on his shoulder. He turns in my direction instantly, his features falling back to normal in the same moment.

"Look, I don't understand what's happening," I say, looking at him before I turn my attention to Natalie. "But you came to me for a reason. If you think I can help, then use me. Aiden is my...trainer." I want to call him so many other things, but this is the safest one. "He's protected me before, and if I can return the favor, then let me."

This sounds a lot more diplomatic than I thought I was capable of. Something flashes in Natalie's eyes, and I wonder if it's a bit of respect. No one ever takes a stand against the shifters. Especially not an alpha. But I'm more scared of Aiden getting hurt than I am of Natalie and what she can do to me. I think she understands that now.

"Fine. Tell me what you know," she says, pulling away her wolf and folding her arms in front of her. I glance at Ben and Owen who are back to normal as well, but they're not moving from their position beside me. I have a feeling they're going to stick even closer to me now.

"I don't know anything; that's the problem. You think I do. So, tell me what you think I know, and we'll go from there. What did you mean he left to help me?"

Natalie rolls her eyes, and at first, I think she'll get into another argument. But after she stretches her arms over her head, she levels me with a glare.

"Your stupid spell, the one that brought us here, he's been researching it as much as he can." That's news to me because he never mentioned that. But instead of admitting that, I have a more important question.

"How would he research such a thing in the forest?"

"You really know nothing of this world, do you?" That makes me angry. Even if I studied for a hundred years, there would still be areas of Faery, and its people that I would not understand.

"How about instead of insulting me every ten seconds, you tell me what you're talking about? It'll save both of us a lot of time," I snap. This conversation could've taken half the time if she'd just get over herself. I get it that she doesn't like me, but for an alpha, she's acting a little too emotional. Not that I can talk. I just had a panic attack.

She rolls her eyes again, and I wonder if she can blink like a normal person, or if that's just what she does. But I don't comment.

"The forest here holds many secrets and many doors. You can wander for a mile and find entrances to many dimensions. But you can also find doors full of knowledge."

"You're telling me Aiden found a door like that?"

"That's what I think. There are creatures living in those woods that have more information than we could ever learn in our life-time. If he stumbled onto one of those, he could be in trouble."

"Because no information is given freely."

"You're not as dumb as you look."

It's my turn to glare at her, but my mind is already lost in thought. If he went into those woods to look for answers, and found someone willing to talk, there's no telling what they would make him do in return. How many times have I told Jade to be careful with her words around the fae? Why would Aiden do something so stupid?

"Why didn't he take one of you with him?" I ask, turning to the other two shifters.

"We always patrolled alone, so we don't raise suspicion," Ben replies, shrugging a little. A part of me wants to yell at them and tell them they should've gone anyway. But I know they won't disobey their alpha.

"Believe it or not, I had no idea Aiden was doing that. The only thing I knew was that he was trying to figure out why we were kept within these boundaries so tightly. But we haven't even discussed that in weeks."

This is probably not what Natalie wanted to hear, but that's the truth. She studies me for a tense moment before shaking her head.

"Well, then you are no help. Not that I'm surprised." I ignore that last remark, and her for that matter, and turn to the boys.

"Could you find his trail? Have you tried?"

"I've tried." Natalie's voice brings me back to her. "It's no use. It ends a little after the hedge. And it gets harder and harder to get past the boundary."

So, there must be magic at work here. Which I guess I already knew. But my mind is full of possibilities. I can work with my magic, that's something I don't fail at on the regular. A tracking spell will be easy to create, especially if I use one of the shifters in front of me as the main ingredient.

"What are you thinking Maddie?" Ben asks, watching my face curiously.

"That I have a way to find him. But I need to ask someone a question first."

"Oh, do you mean your fae friend?" Natalie asks as I turn to head back to the academy. I glance at her sharply as she gives me a pointed look. "Who do you think Aiden used to get through the hedge in the first place?"

"Liam helped him?" I'm not sure I could be any more surprised if I tried. Aiden has a clear dislike of the fae, and yet, here he is working with one. So many questions spring to my mind, and Liam better be ready to answer them. Just as the thought comes to mind, I freeze.

"Wait, when was the last time anyone has seen Aiden?"

"Two days ago," Owen replies, and I try not to visibly react to that. He's been gone for two days, and I had no idea. But then, it comes to me.

"Liam has been gone for that long," I state, and I don't have to explain any further. All three turn their eyes on me, and I meet each gaze one at a time. "We're going after them."

☙❧

WE GET BACK TO THE SCHOOL, SEPARATING AT THE FRONT doors. Each has been given a task, and I have a few hours before nightfall to get my portion of it done. First of all, I need to talk Jade into a) staying and b) covering for me. It won't be easy, considering she told me she's not letting me try any more magic alone.

"Where have you been?" she asks the moment I step into our room. Thankfully, she's alone. I thought maybe Noel and Vera would be in here, but maybe Jade knew I wouldn't talk in front of them. I'm keeping my circle tight, even within my friend group.

"Aiden's missing," I reply, seeing no need to sugar coat it. She opens her mouth, but whatever she was going to say, dies on her lips.

"Are you sure?"

"Positive. And I have a plan for finding him, but I need your help."

"What do you need me to do?" She doesn't even hesitate. For some reason, that brings tears to my eyes, and I step up to her, wrapping her in a tight hug. She holds me back just as tightly as I focus on breathing and not crying. Even though she's not blood, she's become like a sister to me, and her support means the world.

"You're not going to like it," I reply, stepping back.

"I'm one hundred percent sure of that," she says, giving me a quick smile.

"I need you to cover for me. I'm going with the shifters into the forest. That's where Aiden disappeared. I'm going to use one of them as the fuel to my tracking spell."

"You're hoping the pack's bond will help the spell?"

"Exactly." I move toward my closet, pulling out a backpack. I haven't used it since the last time Dad and I went on one of our camping trips. It really seems like another life, one I'm no longer part of. Running my hands over the material, I push the worry away. I can only handle one missing man in my life, at a time. Because this one, I can actually do something about. Quickly, I place essentials in the bag.

"I don't like you not taking me with you," Jade comments from her position on the bed. I knew this was coming.

"You're the only person who can keep my secret, Jade," I say, turning to face her. "I will only be missing Friday classes and then it's the weekend."

"We have an assembly tomorrow. How am I supposed to cover for that?"

That's right. I completely forgot. Headmaster Marković has been holding weekly assemblies to let us know what's going on. Not that he ever tells us anything useful. It's mostly to make people think they're involved and in the know. But most of us are not fooled.

"I don't know. I just know I can't let him stay out there, without even trying to help. He could've gotten himself into a real mess."

I give her a quick run down of everything I learned, and she listens without interruption. For a moment, I think of skipping over my panic attack, but in the end, I don't.

"I have no idea what came over me, or why it was so intense." If anyone can guess, it would be Jade. She's not a Reader, but her intuition hasn't failed us yet. Besides Christie, of course. That girl played her part so well, I think even she believed she was one of us.

"I think it's because you care about him. You can't tell me you two are not connected in some way. I've seen you together."

"No, I can't. But it feels like more."

"And I think you're right. But I can't answer that. The shifters will have to take that one."

"Not that they will tell me. They're being very stubborn."

"Wow, imagine that. Someone being stubborn."

I laugh at that and feel slightly better. Jade does have that effect on me. We kind of balance each other out. And she's definitely knowledgeable enough in magic that she's the perfect person to have on my side.

"What are you thinking?" she asks after I finish packing.

"I need to create a tracking spell, but I won't do it until we're outside the hedge. No need to alert anyone to my intentions." Jade nods at that. I'm especially concerned with Headmaster Marković knowing what I'm up to. He told me once that my magic reads a specific way, and he's been tracking it. It's how he knew I was keeping a secret, even though I can't tell him about the library.

Speaking of that place, it would be very helpful if I could get into it. But I would be foolish to try right now when I'm on such a tight schedule. Also, I don't need it zapping me into unconsciousness.

"What ingredients are you missing?"

I do a quick inventory of everything I have stored up, realizing I'm missing two elements.

"I need barberry root and calamus."

"Miss Lee will for sure have those in her classroom."

Jade's right. We worked with the elements a few months ago. Miss Lee always keeps extra in the closet in her classroom. While we're allowed to be in those rooms after class, everything we do is watched pretty closely. I don't know if we can just walk in and grab them.

"Okay, then I guess we need to sneak in."

❧ 13 ❧

We wait about an hour as I prepare the rest of the ingredients and place them inside my backpack. They need to be separated until the moment I'm putting them together, so I stuff them in different pockets and wrap them in separate sections of my sweater. I don't want any of them to lose their potency.

Once the dinner bell rings, we leave the room with the rest of the students. Owen is in charge of grabbing a few snacks for the trip, since we have no idea how long we'll be gone. There's no doubt in my mind that when we come back, they'll be hell to pay. Especially if the queen finds out about our little adventure. But I'm willing to take that risk for Aiden, and so is his pack.

When Jade and I reach the bottom floor, we follow the rest of the students into the dining room. Ben comes up, and I place a piece of paper in his hand as he says hi and buy. It's a completely normal exchange, so I don't think anyone notices. Once inside, Jade and I wait about a minute standing in line before she clutches her stomach.

"Are you okay?" I ask, adding a note of concern to my tone.

"Help me to the bathroom, please," she replies in mock whisper. Even some of the students who are not shifters have heard our exchange. I place a comforting hand on her arm, and we walk out at a moderate pace, so as to not attract any more attention. We actually walk all the way to the bathroom, and step inside, before Jade stands up normally.

"Now what?"

"Now," I reply, walking farther into the bathroom, "we climb out that window."

Jade looks up at the rectangular window over our heads before she looks at me. While most of the castle has kept its original structure, there were two communal bathrooms built downstairs to help students stay on track between classes. It's a very modern design, complete with the overhead window.

"You're serious?"

"Of course I'm serious. Ben unlocked the window in Miss Lee's class on his way out. We just have to get in there unnoticed."

"Couldn't have Ben also grabbed the ingredients?" Jade asks, coming up to stand beneath the window with me.

"Really? You wanted a shifter to find the right ingredients?"

Jade nods at that because there's no arguing with my logic. I'm not being mean. As witches, we take pride in our work. I'm also nervous about anyone else mixing the ingredients before they get to me. This way, I know they'll be useful.

"Alright. How are we getting up there?" Jade points to the window, and I grin. The window is slightly cracked to let air through, but it's enough.

"Like this."

I take a few steps back, then do a running start, jumping just before I reach the wall. My hands land on the windowsill, and I pull myself up. Satisfied I can do that, I drop back down.

"Wow, someone got strong," Jade comments, and I grin. It's true. Working out with Aiden has made my body more flexible and much stronger than before. I still have curves, but now they're more defined than ever. I'm definitely not complaining.

"Thank you, thank you. Now, I'll boost you up and then follow. Okay?"

"Okay."

Twining my fingers together, I place them down, so Jade can step in with her foot. She does, and I boost her up as she grabs the top. Pulling herself through the opening, I hear a thud and then, "I'm okay."

My turn. I walk a few feet back, redoing the exact same move I did earlier, except now when I grab the windowsill, I pull myself through. When I'm on the other side, I drop and roll, landing in a crouch. After a quick look around, I see that no one is on this side of campus, and I have to be thankful for small favors.

"Come on."

Jade and I stay close to the wall as we race toward the classroom window. Thankfully, the windows are large, as Miss Lee requires extra light for the spells we practice. I cross my fingers, hoping Ben did his part, and when I reach for the bottom of the window, it slides right up.

No one is inside and Jade and I have no problem getting in. I shut the window behind us, just in case anyone looks over and sees it open. We head directly for the large closet at the front of the room when we hear a noise outside.

"Hide," I mouth as we rush toward the closet. There is nowhere else to hide. If it's Miss Lee, she's probably here to do inventory or something like that, so being in the closet is the worst place we can be.

We hear the door open, and we exchange a look. I'm trying to come up with a plausible explanation of why we would be here, but I have nothing. We look guilty.

"Oh hey, Miss Lee." I hear Ben's voice and breathe easier instantly. Motioning for Jade, we start searching through the ingredients. "Can I ask you a random question? It has to do with one of my classes."

"Of course Mr. Light, how can I help?"

The door shuts, and their voices become muffled. It's now or never. My eyes land on calamus, and I grab the bottle just as Jade comes up to me holding a pouch of barberry root. We don't hesitate. Stepping out of the closet, we hurry over to the window, pulling it open quietly. Jade goes first, and I follow quickly, pulling the window closed in the same movement. The door opens in the same motion, and I drop to the ground and out of sight. Jade and I sit on the dirt for a moment longer before we squat and hurry away.

"That was close," she comments, linking her hand through mine.

"But we got it."

Now, I just need to make sure we can get off campus.

WAITING FOR NIGHTFALL IS ABSOLUTE TORTURE. I'M BEYOND restless, and I've been pacing for the last hour. Jade has stopped trying to get me to sit. I know my nervousness is not helping her own. When the bell for lights out finally sounds, it's like the greatest sound in the world.

I have to get out before the lockdown is in place. Jade and I have already said our goodbyes, so I grab my bag and give her a quick wave before I slip out the door. The moment it shuts behind me, it clicks, and I know the spell is in place. Ben mentioned that the spell for the outside doors is a little different, since the patrols have to go in and out. He can get me through, but I have to get there first.

With the added security, it's slow going. The only helpful aspect is a lot of the patrol are fae, and therefore, they don't have shifter's hearing or senses. I can hide behind various structures and statues without being sensed. I just have to be smart about it. A part of me could be worried they'll leave without me, but they have no way of tracking Aiden past the hedge, so I know they'll wait. But with the way I'm moving, they'll have to wait longer than they want.

When I'm finally downstairs, it feels like hours have gone by. I can't take more than a dozen steps before I duck behind a shelf. Glancing around the corner, I see the door to the dining room slightly open. That's where I'm supposed to be meeting Ben. The glass doors that lead out to the yard are the closest to me, besides the front door. There's no way we'd be able to walk out there and make it to the back unseen. I get ready to move again when I hear voices.

Slamming myself back against the wall, I breathe through my nose, hoping it's fae and not shifters on the other side of the hall-way. Shifters can probably hear my accelerated heartbeat as I force it to calm down. After what seems like an eternity, the voices move on, and I breathe a little easier. Peeking my head around the corner, I can't see anyone, so I rush toward the open dining hall door. Slipping inside, I shut it carefully and turn to the darkness.

Without supernatural sight, I can't see anything but the few outlines of the tables and chairs in front of me. Maybe I should call out, but I know that would be stupid of me, so instead, I just wait. When Ben materializes beside me, I'm proud of myself for not jumping. He points down at my hand and I nod, letting him take it. He leads me over to the doors, weaving in and out of the tables without any issues. It takes work to stay close enough to him to follow suit. Once by the doors, he stops, turning to me.

"I'll have to carry you."

The words immediately take me back to when Aiden did so, and I get a chill from the memory. I know it's the only way to merge our supernatural signatures to get through the barrier, but a part of me wants to say no. I don't understand it, but I squish the urge down. This is no time for weirdness. Instead, I step up, nodding my head.

Ben doesn't hesitate to reach over, sweeping me off my feet and into his arms. I wrap my own around his neck, expecting to feel the rush I felt with Aiden. But there's nothing. Ben feels the regular hot of any shifter and smells just as fascinating. But I don't feel anything toward him, not in the way I felt being held in

Aiden's arms. I burrow my head into Ben's shoulder and trust him to get us to the outskirts. The wind comes and is gone before I know it, and the shifter is placing me on the ground, right inside the tree line.

"You okay?" he whispers, and I nod, knowing he can see me. Just then, Natalie and Owen step out of the shadow, their own clothes dark, matching my jacket and jeans.

"Let's get past the hedge," I say, keeping my voice low. I don't have to have supernatural eyesight to see Natalie is annoyed with me as we begin moving. The shifters could get there much faster if they weren't staying beside me, but we have no choice. They need me, and I need them.

My mind goes over every possibility of what could happen and the vast majority of that is not good. We could be caught, we could be killed, we could be put into eternal servitude. This is not an easy path, but I know Aiden would do it for us. He's already doing it for me. It's getting more difficult to keep my emotions at bay, but I refuse to have another panic attack. I'm especially not going to lose it in front of Natalie.

The shifter leads the way, staying a good ten feet in front of us, which means I can't really see her. Ben is beside me, leading me through the darkness, with Owen bringing up the rear. I hate the fact that I'm at a disadvantage, but I can't use magic to help me. Not while I'm on campus. I just hope my magic is enough when we're off it.

It takes us a little over half an hour to get to the hedge. When we finally stop, it seems bigger than I remember. I glance to my right, then to my left, and it seems to go on forever.

"Did it get bigger?" I ask, stopping right in front of it and looking up.

"It did. Bigger and stronger," Owen replies. Makes sense. If they figured out someone has been getting through, it's only normal they would make it a bit harder. It's an interesting type of magic. Harper would love to explore it more, since she's the one in my family with the natural elements affinity. Not that Bri wouldn't love to research it.

"Are you ready?" Ben asks, breaking through my thoughts, for which I am thankful. I can't be getting emotional about my family right now. I need to concentrate.

"Yes."

He takes my hand, and together, we step into the bush.

❦ 14 ❧

The branches seem to fight us for a moment, and I think we'll be stuck in the in-between forever, and then we're through. I stumble, and the only reason I don't face-plant is because Ben's hand is holding mine.

"You good?"

"Yes, thank you," I reply, and that's when I notice I can see him better. Glancing around, I realize the moon shines brighter here than on the other side of the hedge. "We should move a little before I try the spell," I continue. "Can you lead us in the direction Aiden went?" The last is directed at Natalie, and she doesn't reply. Just turns and starts walking away. The air is chilly here, and I'm glad I'm wearing my jacket. The shifters run hotter than the rest of us, in more ways than one, but even they have long sleeves on.

In about five minutes, Natalie stops. Without a word, I drop down to the ground and take out the ingredients one by one. The last item is four tarot cards, each with a corresponding ace to mark the elements. I place those at four corners, indicating North, West, South, and East. Then, I motion for Ben to step in.

"Sit right here while I do this," I say, pointing to the center. Once he's seated, I take out a basil leaf, lighting it as I walk around the circle. Owen and Natalie stand to the side, both on alert and fascinated. It's rare for shifters to watch witches cast big spells. It's kind of like me watching them shift. It's a glimpse into the other world for us. When the circle is cast, I take a seat in front of Ben.

"You ready for this?"

"Absolutely." He gives me a huge grin, and I smile back. Even though I didn't feel any similar feelings toward him when he held me, I realize he's important to me. This spell has a better chance of working because of our connection. The air around me is energized from my circle cast, so it's time.

Placing a small bowl in between us, I call on my water magic, holding my hands over the ground. The magic inside of me stretches, as if it's been laying in one spot for too long before it unfurls around us. Turning my hands palm up, I reach for the moisture in the ground and the plants around us. Drop by drop, the water comes, floating up and toward me as I collect it into small spheres over my hands.

When there is enough, I turn my palms inward, letting the water fall into the bowl. Next, I pick up a basil leaf and a lighter. Burning the leaf, I drop it into the water before reaching for the barberry root. I do the same thing to it before I reach for calamus. After all three have burned, I take out hibiscus. This one, I crush between my hands, and motion for Ben to give me his. I turn his hands palms up before I sprinkle hibiscus bits all over them. Then, I take another petal and burn this one, dropping it into the bowl. Last but not least, I take out sugilite and kyanite, placing each in Ben's hands. Both are strong crystals meant for guidance.

Taking my own hands, I put them over Ben's and close my eyes as I pull on my power. Something strong rises in me, and I want to speak words that are unusual. I realize it's the spell casting trying to break through, and I push it back. I'm not about to make matters worse by performing magic I don't understand. Instead, I look for the knowledge shared with me by my sisters and mother.

This type of spell doesn't require spoken word, just intention. I told Ben to think of finding Aiden, and so I follow suit. For just a

VALIA LIND

moment, the magic within me fights itself before settling on what I want. It brings a smile to my face as I feel it tug at my heartstrings. My magic is like an old friend, and while it was drained for a while, it's always been there. Now, I need it to help me find Aiden.

The bowl between us ignites, evaporating the water and sending a sweet fragrance into the air around us. I open my eyes just as Ben does, our hands hot where they touch.

"How do you feel?" I ask, watching him for any reaction.

"Elated." That brings another smile to my face. His wolf likes my magic, that much I can tell. "And determined." I nod at that before I remove my hands from his.

"Place the crystals into your pockets. They'll help keep the spell at bay. Don't move just yet," I hurry to add when he goes to stand. I jump to my feet, grabbing the cards as I walk in a counterclockwise circle. Once the last card is picked up, I turn to Ben.

"The circle I broken. You can stand now."

He does, and I can tell my magic is all around him. He's watching me with a new kind of intensity, and when I glance at Owen and Natalie, I find their eyes on me as well.

"That was pretty incredible," Owen comments, which means a great deal, coming from a stoic shifter such as him. "Does your skin always glow when you do magic?"

"Not always," I reply and turn back to Ben. "Well, what do you think?"

"I can feel a pull in a certain direction. It definitely reads like Aiden."

"Good. That means my magic is not only pretty, it works." Both of the shifters smile at that while Natalie rolls her eyes. It really is her go to response to everything. I'm finding it comforting at this point. "Can you tell how far he is?"

"He's not close." My heart drops at his words, but I'm not surprised. He would've been found by now if he was close. "We should make camp and then start in the morning."

It's not what any of us want to hear, but Ben is right. Although, with the magic awakened in my veins, I'm not sure how I'll be able to sleep. Especially now that I know Aiden can be found.

Surprisingly, I fall asleep right away. And when I sleep, I dream.

This time, I know I'm dreaming. The fog rolls in just like the last time, but even so, I get a glimpse of my surroundings and realize I'm in the forest. The same forest I just performed the spell in.

Even though the scenery looks familiar, the feeling it evokes is entirely different. My heart beats loudly in my chest, as if making sure I'm aware of the danger. Because nothing feels safe as I stand surrounded by the thick fog.

A noise comes from my left—or maybe it's behind me—and I turn quickly, trying to see if anyone is there. That feeling of being watched comes over me, and I reach for my battle magic. When nothing happens, I almost growl out loud. I forgot my magic doesn't work here, and that makes me so much more afraid.

"What do you want?" I throw my question out into the space around me, hoping for something concrete. Instead of the half answers I got last time. But no answer comes, and I grow more irritated by the minute. If I'm being pulled into this place, there has to be a reason. But so far, all I'm getting out of it is fear. I don't need to be more afraid than I already am. Plenty of things are going wrong in the real world.

"Stop playing games and show yourself!" I yell, no longer caring about decorum. My fear is making me reckless, but at this point, what else am I to do? I know enough about dream walking to know I can be hurt here, if the dream weaver deems it necessary. But I also know I can find a way to control it, if I'm strong enough. I don't pretend to be, but it doesn't mean I'm not going to try.

"Whatever games you're playing, they stop now. What do you want?"

For just a second, I think I made things worse. The air grows heavier around me, the fog thicker. But then, something happens. To my right, the fog parts, and a shadow moves toward me. Everything in me tells me to run, but I stand my ground. Where would I run anyway? It's not my dream, whoever this is, they would be able to find me. When the shadow steps into the light, I gasp.

"Not whom you expected?"

"Not at all," I swallow around my words, "Your Highness."

The queen of Spring Court smiles, but there's no kindness in that. Her sharp teeth seem sharper, her features more striking. Which makes her appear that much more terrifying.

"Do you really think I do not know of the magic you practice over my lands?" She walks around me slowly, like a hunter circling her prey. And that is exactly how I'm feeling standing under her scrutiny. My mind races with the possibilities of a response, but I can't lie to her or make up stories.

"I'm sorry, Your Highness," I say, bowing my head a little before I look up and look her straight in the eye. "I made a mistake, and I brought us here. If I don't do everything in my power to right the wrong, I won't be able to live with myself."

She doesn't respond right away, making another circle around me before finally stopping to face me. The gown she's wearing, a light green, that of fresh leaves springing out from a dormant branch, seems to melt into the fog around her. Everything in this forest is an extension of her, and it was my oversight not to remember that.

"Do you truly believe your magic is a mistake?"

The question surprises me. I expected more reprimands, or even threats, but not an inquiry that makes me pause. Do I believe my magic is a mistake? Even when I'm afraid of it, it's still a part of me. An intricate part that I would not untangle, even if I could.

"No," I reply, facing the queen straight on. She smiles again, and it feels even more dangerous than before.

"Good. While most fear what they do not understand, you must embrace it. The magic brought you here for a reason. Learn that reason and use it."

While her words ring true in my mind, I hear an underlying something between them. She wouldn't be as powerful of a queen if she didn't have her own agenda in every aspect of her life. But how do I ask the necessary questions? It really is not my place. But I know I have to because I need to know at least some of her intentions.

"Is that why you have...asked for my presence for lessons?" My question comes out much stronger than I thought it would. A gleam of approval shines in her eyes before she takes a tiny step forward.

"You are clever enough, Madison Hawthorne, to know I have my own reasons for your magic. I am curious about you and what you are capable of. If your magic can help me defeat the Ancients, then we would be in a very agreeable partnership. Why would I not have your best interest at heart, based on that one truth?"

I get what she's saying, just like she expects me to. She won't reveal her plans, but she does have them. No matter how I spin it, I'm under her thumb. No amount of courage will help me get out of that arrangement. But maybe, just maybe, I can learn how to use her for my own advantage as well.

"Will I be punished?" I dare to ask, knowing full well she's not happy I've broken her rules.

"Maybe. Maybe not," she replies, always the fae. *"Since I have been called away, we have not had our meetings. Finish your quest and return to take a room at the castle. All will be determined then."*

As I try to wrap my mind around her words, she takes a step into the fog, and as it swallows her up, it dissipates. Just as quickly, my head begins spinning, and I'm thrown out of the dream.

Sitting up, I gasp coming awake, and Ben is instantly by my side.

"Maddie, are you okay?" he asks, placing a gentle hand at my back, as if he's afraid I'll topple over. I look up into his worried eyes, noticing it's a little lighter outside.

"The queen knows what we've done," I say, wiping the sweat from my forehead. "She's not happy, but she's not stopping us."

Natalie and Owen come to stand beside us as I speak, and the shifters exchange a look. Now that I think about it, she didn't mention them, so maybe I can protect them from her. If she's tracking my magic, she won't be tracking theirs.

"Well, let's get moving then," Natalie snaps, turning on her heel and heading to the fire we built last night. Ben rubs small circles at my back, and when I glance at him, his eyes are focused on something far away.

"Don't worry," I say, placing a hand on his arm and bringing his attention back to me. "We'll be okay."

"But will you? If anything happens—"

"Nothing will happen. I've got pretty great bodyguards on my side." I give him a smile, and I hear Owen grunt half a laugh. But Ben isn't deterred.

"We can't protect you in your dreams."

That makes me pause, but no matter how true that is, I won't let them take this as their burden.

"Maybe not, but I can protect myself if I know you're watching my back."

My words come out strong, a note of power I don't expect, and it makes even Natalie turn and look at me. She doesn't seem happy with it, but I can tell Ben feels better. There's a gleam of approval in his eyes, and that's all I need. Now, we get to see just how powerful my magic is. I'm ready to find Aiden.

❧ 15 ❧

As we begin our trek, the forest seems restless around us. Or maybe it's just me. I can't shake off the dream, or the feeling of being watched. That last part might have something to do with Natalie throwing glares my way every few minutes. It's as if everything I do makes her hate me more and more. I don't understand her dislike of me in the first place, so it's just getting ridiculous at this point.

Ben stays a few feet in front of me at all times. His shifter senses are mixed with my spell, and so his steps are sure in the direction he's leading. The closer we get, the harder my heart pounds in my chest. I can't pretend I'm not scared for Aiden or worried about what he must be in the midst of. And when I think of Aiden, I think of Liam and get angry all over again. Maybe Aiden wouldn't tell me what he's doing, but Liam and I are friends. While I know he's still a fae, he's always been different with me. So why change now? What has happened to make two complete opposites team up and break the queen's rules? It seems my list of questions will continue to grow, with no answers in sight.

At that moment, Natalie turns and gives me her half glare, half roll of the eyes, and I've had enough. Picking up my speed a tad, I snap.

"What is your problem with me?"

The shifter spins on her heels immediately, and while that's very intimidating, I don't flinch. I have plenty of worries to carry on my shoulders and even more areas to fear. I'm done being scared of her.

"Where do I even start?" she growls, when she sees me not backing down. Ben and Owen move to either side of me, strong pillars of support, but I want to do this myself. Natalie, of course, doesn't miss the gesture. She throws her hands up, pointing at the boys. "This is definitely a good place to start."

I glance at Ben and Owen, my brow furrowed at her meaning. They've always been protective of me, but I don't understand how this concerns her. Then I notice the boys specifically not looking at me directly, and I narrow my eyes.

"What are you not telling me?" I ask Ben, but he stays stubbornly mute.

"Of course they won't tell you. They're not about to disobey their alpha. But I have no qualms about that," Natalie says, smiling a very dangerous smile.

"You will not." Owen surprises me by stepping between the girl and me. His body is tense, and I can see the wolf pushing to the surface. My eye snap to Ben, and he looks just as ready for a fight. This is definitely déjà vu.

"Stop it. All of you." I push between Owen and Ben, so I can see Natalie again. "You, stop sending me dirty looks all the time. You hate me? Cool. Then don't look at me. You two." I point at the boys. "What is with this extra macho intimidation technique? I can protect myself, you know."

"It's not that..."

"We know..."

Ben and Owen speak over each other but stop when Natalie's laugh rings out. All three of us turn in her direction, as she levels us with a glare.

"They can't help themselves," she says, pointing at the boys. Confusion clouds my mind, but no one is offering up any explanations. "But you're not as much of a weakling as I thought you were, so I'll give you that."

She turns then, continuing to walk through the forest as if nothing has happened. I glance at the boys, but they won't be sharing any time soon. Ben hurries to take the lead, with Owen falling into step behind me.

My sisters have told me the range of a shifter's emotion. They can go from hot to cold in the span of a second. Their tempers are not something to be trifled with, and I'm sure if my family could see me now, they'd be telling me to back off. But I can't shake the feeling that all three of them are keeping something incredibly vital from me. I felt it when Natalie first attacked me, and I feel it now. But since it clearly has something to do with Aiden, I guess I'll have to wait and ask him myself.

At least Natalie seems to have stopped throwing dirty looks my way. We've been walking for an hour, and she's only looked at me once. Suddenly, Ben stops, his eyes focused on something I can't see. I come up to stand beside him as Natalie and Owen follow suit.

"What is it?"

"There's a small village in front of us," Ben says as Owen nods. Their eyesight is truly awesome. "Aiden's signature is all over it. It's the strongest I've felt."

My heart leaps in my chest at those words, and I try to contain my excitement. We're getting closer. I have no idea how far from the academy we've gone, but the spell has clearly broken through the confusion barrier placed around the school's campus. Even after half a day, I wasn't so sure. But now I am and so are the shifters.

"Not bad, witch," Natalie says as she takes off toward the village. Halfway through the run, she shifts, her clothes disappearing into the shift. Even Aiden doesn't have that capability yet, and I wonder who spelled her to carry the clothes with her.

"She'll recon," Ben comments, turning to me. "Then we'll follow suit."

I nod, trying to keep my excitement at bay. We're getting closer.

☙☞

While we wait for Natalie to return, I can't keep still. The pacing I've become so fond of has returned, and I think it's making the guys a little annoyed. I keep making noise every time I step on a crunchy leaf, but I can't help myself.

"You know, if you sat in one spot, we would be less likely to get noticed," Owen points out after another five minutes of my frantic movement. Did I call it, or did I call it?

"Yes, but—"

"Maddie, we're all feeling it. But we have to stay calm."

"I am calm. Don't I seem calm?" I ask as I make another pass in front of the shifters. My question makes Ben chuckle, so I stop moving and turn to him. "Sorry, I'm just..."

"We get it. We're close. Either Aiden is there or he's nearby."

For some reason, when Owen says that, it makes me think he means something more than the words he speaks. I'm back to that secret they're keeping from me, but even though Natalie isn't here, I doubt they'll tell me. After all, she's the one who would've, and they keep stopping her. Even so, I open my mouth to speak, but then freeze. Something changes in the air, an intensity that wasn't there before.

"Guys," I whisper and then they're on their feet. They sense it too if their wolf is any indication. Both have opened up a pathway into the shift but haven't taken the leap yet. I've seen them do this a few times already, but it still fascinates me. Their eyes turn gold or silver, depending on their wolf, and their features get a soft gaze of an outline around them. It's as if they're on the edge, and all they have to do is plunge forward to fully become wolves.

"Stay between us, Maddie," Ben commands, not taking his eyes off our surroundings. I bristle at that a little, my battle magic sizzling at my fingertips immediately.

"I'm not so helpless," I say just as a movement to the left catches my eye. Something darts in the trees beyond our mini-camp, and I try to follow it as I turn, but it's moving too fast. "What is it?" I ask, hoping the shifter's senses have picked it up. I'm not disappointed.

"It's a troll." Owen says just as it attacks. It's not like any troll I've ever studied. This is more rabid, a short and quick creature, and it's on a mission to destroy without a conversation first.

There is more than one, and they descend from the trees. The creatures drop on the ground in front of us, teeth bared. I've never seen them in real life before, and for a second, all I can do is stare. Then, the closest to me launches himself in my direction, but even as I bring my battle magic up, Owen snatches him from the air. With his teeth. He's fully a wolf now, a gorgeous silver beast, coming up to my waist. Twisting around, I see that Ben stayed in his human form, but he's fast enough that he's dodging the creatures.

Another group of five trolls jump from the trees, but this time I'm ready. I raise my hands from the ground up, and a blast of thunder sweeps the creatures right off their feet and into the air. This time, I sweep my hands from over my head to the ground, and the creatures fly back into the trees, knocking a few over. Calling on my element, a stream of water bursts from the ground before expanding into a line and sweeping the creatures on my left off their feet. Ben and Owen are each holding their own, but I'm not beyond helping.

Pulling the water at the top of my hands into orbs, I thrust them one at a time at the trolls. The impact sends them flying, dropping to the ground or ending up back in the trees. My body feels exhilarated, nearly bursting at the seams with power, and I don't want to stop. It's like a door has opened up inside of me and everything is pouring out. It's been so long since I've felt this in-tune with my magic. It's like I found whatever was preventing the flow and ripped it away.

Another blast and the creature hurry away, dragging their

wounded ones behind them. My first instinct is to go after them, but I make myself pause and think. This is not why we've come here. The moment of clarity pulls my magic in, snapping it like a rubber band. My chest feels like it's not big enough to hold it all in. Bending over, I try to breathe, exhausted and exhilarated at the same time.

"Wow, Maddie," Ben says, coming up to stand beside me. "That was impressive."

"Indeed, it was." Natalie's voice sounds as she steps through the trees, two fae coming up behind her. "Impressive enough that you've convinced the villagers to let us in." She motions to the two following behind her and they step forward.

"Thank you for protecting our borders." They bow, and I glance at the shifter smirking beside them. This is not what I expected.

❧ 16 ❦

This trip is not at all what I thought it would be.

"What are they?" I ask as we take a seat at the table in the tavern. The village is more like a small town. Smaller than Hawthorne but still big enough to house all the amenities. The tavern is one of the biggest buildings, with accommodations for travelers in the upstairs rooms. It's very old-timey but still modern enough that I know we haven't stepped into a fairy tale book. The fae may not have all the conveniences, but they stay up on the times. Considering most of the time, a day in the human realm is like ten years here, and vice versa, depending on the magic. I'm intrigued by the way they adapt.

"Trolls." One of the fae who came to meet us on the outskirts speaks up. His name is Hector, and the woman with him is Alvina. Natalie's recon didn't provide any answers, so she made the executive decision to just waltz into their place of business and ask questions. The art of subtlety is clearly lost on her. But at least it seems to have delivered some results.

"They've been terrorizing our borders for months. The queen was to send soldiers to clean up the woods, but with the war on the Ancients, all resources are being sent there instead."

"A war?" That takes me by surprise. I knew the Ancients were right on the borders, but if they've broken in somewhere, the danger is much closer than I thought.

"It's not just in Spring Court," Alvina says. "All over Faery, creatures we've never seen before are rising up. And those we have seen are meaner and bolder in their attacks. We've always had a troll problem, but it's become a real issue recently."

"We're glad we could be of help," Ben says, his tone diplomatic. It's not like we don't care about the plight of these individuals, but there's nothing more we can do.

"We appreciate it. So, we will return the favor," Hector says, turning to face me once again. I realize then that Liam must've sworn them to secrecy. But since we have done them a service, the magic can be overridden. I'm guessing, of course, but it's the best I have from all the research I've done. When I find Liam, I definitely have some extra questions to ask him.

"A Fae of the royal blood came by with a companion. They have gone to see the oracle in the mountains. That is all we can tell you."

My heart leaps at the words. Liam and Aiden were here. There's no one else who could fit that description. But the mountains? I didn't even know there were mountains anywhere close by.

"I understand," I reply, trying to keep my voice calm and collected. "Would you be able to point us in the right direction?"

The fae exchange a look, and I know their answer before they even speak it.

"We cannot. But the oracle is well known around these parts."

"Can't you just—" Natalie snaps, and she seems ready to launch herself at the two across the table. Not that I fault her. I'm not fond of fae games, but they told us what we needed to know.

"It's okay, Natalie." I interrupt her, receiving a scalding look for my efforts. "We'll find the oracle just fine. We would like a room for the night."

Alvina nods before she stands and motions for us to follow. The boys don't question me, but I can see Natalie wants to. Once Alvina shows us to a room, I take out three silver coins and hand them to her. She nods, accepting the payment without audibly saying thanks, and leaves.

"How come the fae never say thank you?" Natalie grumbles as she drops herself onto one of the beds. There are only two in the room, but the place is modern and clean, so I'm not complaining.

"Because everything is a contract here. Even simple gratitude," I reply as I walk over to the window.

"You sure know a lot about fae, witch."

I turn at that, leveling her with a stare. "And you don't know enough, shifter." She rises at that, as if she's going to attack, but I'm not done. "They're bound to keep Liam and Aiden's secret. But they told us the oracle is well known. It means we can ask someone else."

Natalie huffs at that before laying back down. I turn to look out the window. We're on the fourth floor, so I can see over some of the rooftops. The trees here are so old, they reach nearly to the sky. I can't see a mountain anywhere near us, but that doesn't mean one is not there.

"Tomorrow we ask around, carefully, and we'll take it from there." I say, moving away from the window and toward the other bed. There's no way Natalie and I are sharing. She'll probably smother me in my sleep. But it's been a long few days, and I'm sure they didn't get much sleep last night in the woods.

Ben comes to stand near the bed, and I nod. Owen surprises me by walking over to the other side of the room and settling in a chair.

"Aren't you tired?" I ask, and he gives me a rare smile.

"I'll sleep better over here."

Natalie rolls her eyes but doesn't comment as she rolls away from us and presumably goes to sleep. Ben settles onto the bed beside me, and I can't say that it feels strange. I smile down at him as I sit up cross-legged on my side of the bed.

"What are you doing?"

"Making sure we sleep."

Then, I close my eyes and call on my magic. Now that the

adrenaline is gone, the magic feels a little drowsy, like it did after I spell casted. Liam has been worried about the effects, but I haven't given them much thought until now. Maybe something *is* off about my magic. But I can't concentrate on that now. Instead, I call on a protection spell, sending it into the walls, the floor, and ceiling of our room. When that's done, I open my eyes and lay down.

"Thank you, Maddie," Ben whispers before he too gives into slumber. My own sleep doesn't follow as easily.

AFTER I TOSS AND TURN FOR HOURS, LIGHT FINALLY MANAGES TO creep into the room. Thankfully, no one else has suffered from insomnia. I have no explanation as to why I slept in the woods, and I couldn't sleep here.

Actually, as we wash up and head downstairs, I realize it may have something to do with the queen. There were no dreams this time. She's leaving me on my own. I'm not sure if I should be pleased about that or not.

Once downstairs, we don't sit to eat but grab items to go. Contrary to popular belief, most things are okay to eat in Faery. There are only certain foods that should not be consumed by outsiders, and that was the first lesson I learned when I became friends with Liam. He wanted to make sure I was prepared, just in case.

"Where to?" Ben asks as we eat our biscuits. I'm sure the shifters would like something more substantial, but no one complains. Not even Natalie.

"The market?" I reply, looking down the street at what I think is an outdoor bazaar. "There are usually people there who will talk. For the right price."

"Aren't you so smart?" Natalie mumbles before pushing past us and leading the way.

"She's so pleasant in the morning," I comment and watch her

shoulders tighten. But she doesn't turn around. Ben, however, chuckles. We hurry to catch up, and even though the boys seem more relaxed than Natalie, I don't miss the way their eyes keep moving, studying everything in our surroundings. They may handle themselves a bit better, but they're still on high alert, and for that I am thankful. Even though my senses seem to be more attuned to danger, the shifters have a much better idea when something is close by.

The market is in full swing. Everywhere I look, there is someone bartering for goods or services. We push through a throng of people, and I try and find someone who would be willing to talk. Without me having to give up my right kidney. Then, I see her.

The moment my eyes land on the older woman, I don't hesitate to walk over to her. Ben stays close behind with Owen bringing up the rear. When we reach the small booth, I glance down at the array of crystals in front of me.

"Are you looking for something in particular?" the old woman asks, bringing my eyes back to her. Somehow, she looks different from the others here. There's a softness about her that isn't usually found in fae. Or other creatures residing in Faery.

"We are looking for the oracle who lives in the mountains. Would someone be able to show us the way?" I ask, carefully choosing my words. The old woman studies me for a moment before she replies.

"You aren't of this world."

"Neither are you." I guess, but I know I'm right immediately. Ben and Owen both swivel to look at the woman as she gives me a small smile.

"You're an intuitive child. What do you have to do with the oracle?"

"We're looking for our...companions." Even though she's not from here, I still need to be careful. She has clearly lived here long enough to know the dangers of this world. To survive, I'm sure she's adapted.

"We will not make a bargain," I continue, "but will pay a sum upfront."

She studies me again, this time, with a new kind of respect in her eyes. Maybe she expected me to not know what to say or do, but I'm glad Liam made sure to teach me the basics. Even though I'm a bit mad at him still, he might eventually get a thank you from me.

"You are a smart one as well," the old woman comments, standing up from her stool. She's not as tall as I thought she'd be, which solidifies my earlier assessment of her not being fae. "Very well. The mountain you seek is beyond that tree line, about a half-day's walk. Trolls and goblins reside there. Along with other creatures."

"How do we find the oracle once we reach the mountain?"

"If you reach the mountain, the oracle will come to you."

The if does not go unnoticed. I take out five silver coins, handing them over. It might be a little steep to pay for the information we received, but I feel for her. She's in a world that is not her own. Although, maybe I shouldn't be feeling sorry for her at all. She seems to be doing just fine.

"You are generous and kind. Both of those are characteristics the fae will use against you. There are no guarantees with them. Not even the ones who show you kindness."

She doesn't wait for a response but takes the coins and walks back to her stool. It's a warning, but also, I think it's a bit of her own history in those words. I don't say thank you as I turn to leave. We take three steps, and Natalie materializes beside us.

"How many of those coins you got?" she asks, nodding her head toward the stand we just left.

"Not too many," I reply, without giving her specifics. They were a gift from Liam after we became friends. He told me I could use them when I came to visit, and we'd go to the market. It never happened, but I'm glad I kept them safe. From what I know, I could've paid with magic. But that's not something I have stored up at the moment.

We head out of the town without a backwards glance. There's no time to waste now that we know where we're heading. Ben fills Natalie in on what we learned, and all I get is another roll of the eyes. The shifter is beautiful, and I'd like to say her negative attitude makes her less so. But it doesn't. She's exotic in every way, while I feel gross after all the walking we've been doing.

I have no idea why my mind has gone to such trivial things. Maybe it's because I'll be seeing Aiden soon.

❧ 17 ☙

This part of the forest is much darker than the one we left behind. The village woman's words echo in my head as I study our surroundings. My battle magic is brewing under my skin, ready to be released at any moment. The shifters are all on high alert, their bodies tense. We walk steadily, but not too fast. We wouldn't want to attract any unnecessary attention.

After a while, it seems that maybe the woman was exaggerating. But then, I realize just how quiet it's gotten. Ben and Owen both move in closer, and even Natalie slows down to create a tight circle between the four of us. When the first shadow darts between the trees, my heart skips a beat. And not in an exciting way. There's another movement to our right, and this time, my magic comes a little closer to the surface. I'm expecting an attack at any moment, but it doesn't come.

"What's happening?" Natalie asks, keeping her eyes trained on the small bodies jumping around the outside of our perimeter.

"I think they're following us," I reply, confused by the whole situation. They stay close enough that we have to stay in a tight group as we move forward, but they don't come any closer. If the creatures are really so bad, they wouldn't be passing up an opportunity to attack. But while the trolls had no problem with it, these little guys are just observing.

"Why would the woman tell us of the danger if there was none?" It's Ben's turn to ask questions, and this time I do look over at him.

"I don't think she was lying," I reply honestly. "Maybe they're reacting differently to us for some reason."

"Or maybe the woman spun tails so she could get more money off you." Natalie smirks, flipping her hair over her shoulder. Even after days, it's still raven black and silky smooth. My hand automatically reaches for my own hair, but I drop it down. It's fine in the braid it's in. What is wrong with me? I need to focus on the issue at hand, and while I think over Natalie's words, I don't agree with them.

"No," I state, receiving a mild grunt in response. "My instincts are telling me she told the truth. Something else is in play here."

"Oh good. We're relying on her instincts now."

I don't get a chance to response as Ben growls, speeding his walk up a bit to catch up to Natalie. Without thinking, I react, running to grab his arm and pull him back.

"My instincts have gotten us this far," I say, squeezing Ben's arm in warning. "You have a problem, you know the way back." Natalie throws some daggers with her eyes at me, but she doesn't comment further.

Truth be told, she's not the only one frustrated. We're constantly playing catchup in this world, and I'm not seeing us getting ahead any time soon. We need to be ahead if we're going to find Aiden and Liam. Or get out of Faery. But that last one, it's truly on me.

"Wait, do you hear that." I pull on the arm I'm still holding, and Ben immediately stops, looking down at me.

"I hear..."

"Water."

The moment I acknowledge it, I feel it. My heartbeat speeds up in anticipation, and I forget all about the creatures in the forest or the danger they bring. My steps speed up, and in a manner of minutes, we're bursting through the trees, a glorious sight in front of me.

A river of clearest blue flows from east to west, separating this side of the forest from the mountain.

"Look!" I point at the giant rock in front of us as if the shifters can't see it. My heart longs for what's out there, but it also longs for the water. I glance down to the river again, the magic dancing at my fingertips. A noise comes from behind us, and we turn to see goblins on the trees, slapping the bark in excitement as their pointy teeth stick out in huge smiles.

"They weren't trying to hurt us," Owen comments.

"No, they were leading us here."

Without another thought, I walk toward the river. When we're on the bank, Ben tries to reach for me, but Owen stops him, as if he too wants to see what I'm about to do. I don't even know what I'm about to do.

It's been so long since I completely immersed myself in my water magic. Sure, I used some on our little adventure. But before then, the last time I can remember is when I lifted the pond straight in the air and then brought the storm. I've been so busy trying to learn this new power inside of me, I've completely neglected the one I already have.

Stopping right on the bank, I lift my arms, stretching them in front of me, palms up. The river rushes by beneath me and I can feel its rhythm like the beating of a heart. Closing my eyes, I call on my magic, and it answers immediately. Everything I've felt in the past few weeks pours out of me, carried by the power inside me.

A gust of wind kisses my cheeks, and when I open my eyes, the river is dancing in the space in front of me. Snakes slithering over the top of the blue liquid, flowers blooming the size of a small horse, bunnies jumping up and down, trying to reach the butterflies fluttering in the air. Each and every one of them made out of the water living in the river. I've never shaped so fully and effortlessly before, and it takes my breath away. I weave my hands up and down in the air, and the water follows, as if it's desperate for direction. A laugh bubbles inside of me, and I let it out, sending the river into the sky like a million stars. Then, just as it suspends above us, I pull it all in, dropping it back into the riverbank.

My heart beats fast and feels lighter. I turn to look at the shifters who have all been standing completely still as they watched my display. Complete and total awe is written all over their faces. Even Natalie looks impressed. But then, just as I register that, her eyes move over my shoulder, and her expression changes to one of surprise. I twist, and there they stand. Aiden, Liam, and a woman who looks to be in her twenties.

"Now that's what I call a welcoming sight," she says, smiling.

I CAN'T STOP STARING AT AIDEN. IT'S AS IF NOW THAT I'VE LAID eyes on him, all the weirdness I've been feeling has lifted, and I'm finally balanced again. The moment that thought solidifies in my mind, I snap out of it. This is definitely not allowed, and here I am, gaping at him like a lovesick kid with a first time-crush.

Forcing my eyes to shift, I glance at Liam. That's when I notice both of the boys look happy to see me for about a spilt second before that look turns to fear. The woman between them keeps smiling.

"What are you doing here?" Liam's voice snaps me back to myself, and I glance at him to find his expression full of panic before the mask falls back into place. I'm instantly on alert, even though I keep my face as neutral as possible. I'm not as good as it as these boys, but I try.

"You've been missing for days. We've come to bring you home," I reply, grateful that my voice comes out strong and sure. The woman standing between the guys hasn't stopped watching me the whole time, a pleased smile on her face. I find it unnerving.

"Unfortunately for you, little witch," she says, her voice

melodic and soothing. "These two are unable to accompany you back."

"What does that mean?" Natalie growls over the woman's voice, not even bothering to keep the hostility out of her question. She's taken on the persona of a protector, and I wonder if that's how mates work in the shifter world. She's ready to go to battle for Aiden.

Even though my eyes want to drift his way, I keep them trained on the woman. I'm not naïve enough to not realize the danger around her, cloaked in fine beauty. As I study her, I stand by my first impression, she is striking. But she also looks like a sorority sister dressed for a themed party. While a lot of the fae prefer their hair long, hers is cropped right above her shoulders and arranged in a messy bob. Her dress, while full and shiny, is made of something tougher than silk. The green of the dress dances and sparkles every time she breathes.

"It means that nothing is free here and these two," she waves her hand absentmindedly, "have made their choice."

My heart drops in my chest, blood running cold. There's no way they made some kind of bargain. They wouldn't be so foolish. But as I glance over at them, I realize that's what they feared. Me finding out and doing something about it. Well, good on them. They seem to know me well.

"What. Does. That. Mean?" I snap, taking a dangerous step toward the river. The woman's eyes flash in my direction, and I feel movement at my back. Out of the corner of my eye, I see Ben has moved closer to my side, his body rigid.

The woman doesn't miss a thing. She studies those around me before her cold eyes come to rest on me once more. It takes everything in me, but I don't flinch away, holding her gaze as steadily as possible. Suddenly, her melodic laugh rings out around us, making me jump a little.

"You are not what you seem," she states as she waves her hand in front of her. Roots spring from the ground, weaving together as they reach our side of the river. In less than a minute, an intricate pattern emerges, making a solid bridge between us. Instinctually, I take a step back as she moves across the walkway. With my hand at my side, battle magic sparks at my fingertips, and even though it's not visible, her eyes immediately go there.

"Not at all," she murmurs as she steps off the bridge and onto our side of the river. Both Owen and Ben are at my side, just as focused on the woman as I am. Natalie is on the other side of Ben, having a difficult time holding her shift. I glance at her, knowing I have to do something before she loses it and ruins everything.

"Nat, stand down." My voice is low, but her shifter hearing picks it up no problem, as her angry eyes swing toward me. She doesn't like me, and she has no problem showing me that. But for some reason, she listens. As if my words carry more weight than expected, her wolf settles, but she's doesn't break out of her ready stance.

When I turn back to the woman, Liam and Aiden have joined her on our side of the river. It takes much of my self-control not to rush over to them and either hug them or strangle them. I'm not sure when I've become this person, but here we are. I'm not the only one surprised by my leadership. The boys both wear surprised expressions on their faces, and I'm sure it has all to do with the fact that Natalie just listened to me.

"You are a curious creature, little witch." The woman speaks again, her eyes on me like I'm some science experiment waiting to be dissected. She still hasn't answered my question, but it's not like I actually expect her to listen to anything I have to say. I'm trying anyway.

"What's so curious about me?"

"There is powerful magic in your blood. Yet, so unlearned."

"So I keep hearing," I grumble, receiving a slight growl from Aiden. He seems to be even more worked up than Natalie, but he's controlling it much better. I can tell because I've seen him in battle. This is another step above that.

"This is a good place to learn." The woman smiles, but there's no kindness in her eyes. For some reason, I think she means to learn with her. So, I play the only card I have.

"Her Highness Queen Amaryllis has taken it upon herself to teach me," I say, holding the woman's eyes steadily. Gasps sounds from all around me, but I'm not sure if they're shocked or if it's all in my head. The woman's eyes flash, and a part of me thinks the hatred I see there is directed at the Spring Court's queen.

"Of course she has," the woman says, her words dripping with coldness. "But there is something I have that you want." She inclines her head toward the boys. "You and I still have a bargain to make."

"No!" That comes from Aiden, and he moves forward until Liam grabs him and pulls him back. Pushing them from my mind, I focus entirely on the woman. She wants something from me, that's clear as day. And if Aiden and Liam are stuck here, then I have to be willing to do whatever it takes to get them out. No matter how much I hate breaking the number one rule of dealing with the fae.

"What kind of a bargain?"

❧ 18 ❧

"**M**addie, no." Both Liam and Aiden speak, but the woman waves her hand and both their mouths are shut. They struggle against the magic, but it's too powerful to overcome. It's hard not to look in their direction, but I manage. Because this is between me and the woman. I'll deal with them later.

"They came here for information and therefore, I require some as a trade," the woman says, coming to stand just a few feet in front of me. Ben and Owen automatically go to move toward me but can't. I glance at them and see their feet have been swallowed by the grass we're standing in, roots growing over them. Natalie is in the same predicament. How do I stand up to this kind of a power? Fear threatens to overwhelm me, but I search for every lesson, every single word I've ever heard on how not to let it control you, looking for that center. I focus on my breathing, keeping a mental count in my mind, until my mind is settled. The woman doesn't continue, and maybe it's because she's waiting for me to say something.

"What information?" I ask.

"On you, of course. You are an interesting creature, born of past and present. Do you know why your magic brought you to the Spring Court?"

The random question throws me off. Maybe this is just a tactic to keep me on edge, but it's working. The magic inside me is in uproar, scared and ready for battle at the same time. I blink my eyes a few times before I shake my head.

"Spring Court has an affinity to water, the element that fuels everything. You were drawn to it because of your friend." She flicks her hand in Liam's direction. "And your magic was drawn to it because of the power it holds."

If this is the information I'm supposed to be bargaining for, why is she giving it to me freely? Something is missing here, something she's not telling me, and I don't understand how I play into any of this.

"What does it mean?"

"It means you are in the perfect place to learn."

How many times am I going to hear this? Learn, learn, learn. Yet, no one is teaching me anything! Okay, the academy is still teaching me something, but it's not the same. Why are the two most powerful fae I've met so stuck on this one word?

"I can see your frustration, little witch," the woman continues, and honestly, at this point, I think she just likes the sound of her own voice. If I let her fill the silence, maybe she'll give me more than she wants. Not that I actually think that'd work on a master of trickery. It would in the human world for sure.

"Then help me understand," I dare to say. It's not a question but more of a challenge. She studies me again, this time with an intensity that makes me feel like she's looking straight into my soul. My skin prickles under her gaze, and it takes everything in me not to fidget. I can't let myself display any uncertainty. Not when a hunter is looking at me like I'm prey.

"You are to owe me a spell," she finally says, once again choosing what she shares with me. "When I call upon you, you will deliver. A spell of your own particular magic, no questions asked."

I know what she's asking. Somehow, she knows of my story

spell casting, and she wants that power for herself. Making this kind of deal, it goes against everything I know. Even though I'm not looking at them, I can feel Aiden and Liam's eyes on me. They're pleading with me not to make the bargain, but I have no choice. I'm not leaving them here. My mind races over all the knowledge I have on contracts with the fae, and then my father's voice comes into my mind. He's been the Watcher of our coven for years, with his family in the position for generations. Watchers are the history keepers and the mediators between supernatural creatures. I realize he has taught me a lot more about the way of the words than I've thought until now.

"You are to give me the information promised to both Liam and Aiden." I speak up, keeping my voice clear and direct. My eyes are on the woman only, a burst of courage burning in my veins. "Along with whatever you were going to keep to yourself as leverage. Once I am satisfied with the knowledge, and you have released Liam and Aiden from their bargain, you will receive the promise of a spell, executed by me of my own magic. There will be no strings attached now or ever."

I link my fingers in front of me, my shoulders back as I look her in the eyes. This time, there's no doubt of the fleeting approval in her. The boys struggle against their magical bonds behind her, mumbling something around their closed mouths, but it doesn't matter. I have spoken.

"I accept," the woman replies, waving her hand in the air between us. I hear a pop and then, before I can ask anything else, she steps forward, placing her hand against my temple.

A rush of magic bursts into me, making my head spin. It feels like I'm being ripped apart from the inside out, and I grit my teeth against the agonizing pain. Tumbling and spinning, the magic takes me on a ride. Even though a part of me knows I'm still in one place, it doesn't feel like it. When images begin to assault my mind, I can't hold back the screaming any longer.

The only reason I stay standing is by the power of her magic. The only sound I hear is my own voice, going hoarse with exertion.

And then, just as fast as it began, it ends. The woman takes one long look into my eyes and steps back.

Having nothing to hold me up, I drop to the ground, completely exhausted and then everything goes black.

◐✵◑

WHEN I COME TO, THREE PAIRS OF EYES ARE HOVERING OVER me. Ben and Liam look concerned. Aiden looks angry. Raising myself to my elbow, Liam hurries to guide me up, keeping his hand on my back for support. I glance around, but the woman is gone. Owen is on my right and Natalie on my left, their eyes on the surroundings.

"Welcome back, Sleeping Beauty," Natalie mumbles without turning around. I roll my eyes but don't engage.

"How long was I out?" I ask instead.

"About fifteen minutes," Liam replies, rubbing my back in a comforting circular motion. His magic seeps into my skin, helping rejuvenate me. All fae carry a bit of healer magic in them, since they're so closely attuned to the nature around them. Right now, I'm thankful.

"Where is she?"

"She disappeared the moment you passed out. Which is when she freed us as well."

I look over at Aiden, who still hasn't said anything, but I can tell he's mad at me. The feeling is mutual right now, so I make sure to send a glare his way. That seems to rile him up even further.

"Let me up," I mumble when Liam continues to hover. Before I can even begin moving, Aiden is there, reaching to lift me up, but I bat his hands away. He growls a little but doesn't press.

"I can stand on my own," I snap in response as I run my hands over my shirt to smooth it.

"Oh, can you? Can you actually do anything on your own? Like make good decisions?" His eyes are dangerously dark, and I can tell he's barely restringing his wolf right now. But for some reason, I'm not afraid of him. Instead, I move toward him, and when Ben reaches over to stop me, I push his hand away.

"A thank you would be appreciated."

"I didn't ask you to come. You should've stayed at the academy."

"And leave you rotting away in the service of the fae?" My hands move to my hips as I stare the shifter down. I have grown a lot in the past few months, and I have never felt it more than I do at this exact moment. The me from before this ordeal would never have stood up to a shifter this way, much less an alpha. But I'm not afraid of Aiden hurting me. Not physically at least. What I am afraid of is him getting himself killed.

"We would've gotten out on our own," Aiden replies, clearly just as angry as I am.

"When? In a hundred years? What were you thinking?" He opens his mouth to reply, but I'm already turning, this time entirely focused on Liam. "And you! You know better. You know better than all of us. Why would you do this?"

My voice has risen enough to be heard in the forest at my back. Even the pack has moved back, trying to stay out of my way. My body is vibrating with pent up energy, mixed with magic, and I'm breathing heavily. I'm provoking two creatures who are much stronger than I, but it doesn't stop me. Real terror grips my heart at the thought of either of them getting hurt.

"Maddie, you don't understand."

"Then, you better explain it to me!"

"We did it for you!" Aiden snaps, and I twist, staring at him as if I've never seen him before. There's so much in his look I can't even begin to understand, but as he says the words, images of what the woman showed me start falling into place.

"No," I whisper, all energy leaving me as I process the information. It's as if she put it all in my head, but until I made a conscious thought to think about it, it didn't come. Now, it's filling me up with knowledge, and that knowledge feels like a ton of bricks sitting on my chest. Liam and Aiden move toward me as one, grabbing my arms as I sway on my feet. "It's not possible."

"I'm afraid it is."

Raising my head, I stare at Liam, at the uncharacteristic sorrow in his eyes. Fae are not emotionless. I've known that my whole life. But they do control their emotions better than anyone else in this realm or the next. For someone in his position to express so much of it on his face makes all of this worse somehow.

"Did you know before this?" I ask, regaining a little of my strength.

"No."

"What are they talking about?" Ben's voice reaches me, and I look over to see him and Owen hovering nearby. I feel a feather of a touch on my cheek and turn in time to see Aiden wiping a tear from my skin. I'm crying, and I didn't even realize it.

"Maddie?"

"My dad." I hiccup over the words. "My dad is in Faery. It wasn't the Ancients who took him. It was the Winter court."

Whatever I thought, whatever I was going to do, all of it fades away as I come to terms with that information. It's what she told the boys; I know that from the images. But she also kept something from them, a prediction she foresaw. My chest fills with so much pain, I can hardly breathe. Before I know it, Liam is pulling me into his arms, and I cling to him like a lifeline.

"Maddie?" his voice whispers over my head, and I hear it rumble in my ear. I don't want to appear weak in front of any of them, but for just this moment, I let myself feel it all. Before I have to face them. Because I do have to face them, and I have to tell them what's coming.

Pushing away from Liam, I wipe at my eyes and straighten my shirt. Taking a deep breath, I roll my shoulders, compartmentalizing everything I've learned. My dad always said nothing is given to a person that cannot be handled. I've always been stronger than I've given myself credit for, and now, I guess I get to see if my dad was right.

"Dad." My voice catches, and I clear my throat before looking up again. "My dad is being held prisoner in the Winter court, and there is nothing I can do about it right now." Liam reaches for me again, but I wave him away. "What the woman did not tell you..." I glance at him, then at Aiden, who has moved to stand with his pack.

"She did not tell you the Ancients aren't the only evil at the borders. A plague has spread throughout Faery, and it is now on the threshold of Spring." The group exchanges glances as I take another pause. "We're in real trouble here."

And once again, it is all my fault.

𝕾 19 𝕾

Everyone has questions. Even Natalie steps forward after staying quiet for so long.

"We don't have time for this," I interrupt, putting my hand up. I gave them a little longer than I had, so it seems fair. "We have to get back, and we have to warn Headmaster Marković."

"What exactly is happening?" Aiden may still be angry at me—right back at ya buddy—but he's all business now. There's the alpha I know and...*nevermind*.

"When I figure out how to sort through all the information she stuck in my head, I'll let you know. But for now, we need to go."

No one can argue with that logic. I glance behind us at the spot where the bridge of thorns was and wonder what kind of a spell she will require of me. For someone as powerful as she is, why bother with my minuscule spell work? Not that I can do anything about it now. One way or another, I did what I came here to do. I got Liam and Aiden back. I don't care if they're not happy with me.

It doesn't take us long to get back to the village. I scan the area for the older woman we met, but the bazaar is gone. Since we've spent most of the day getting there and back, the sky has grown dark, so we head toward the hotel we stayed at last time. Alvina meets us at the bar, a small smile on her face.

"I knew you'd be back," she calls in greeting before her eyes move over the rest of the group. "And you found your companions."

"Something like that," I reply as Hector comes out from the back. "We would like a room for the night."

"Not a problem." The two exchange a look before Alvina motions us to follow her, like before.

Alvina leads us to the same room we were in before, and this time it's Liam who pays her. Everyone goes to their corners while Natalie follows Aiden to the bed. She's been trying to get him to talk to her, but he's not in the mood. From my position on the other side of the room, I watch as she reaches over, running her hand gently over his hair, neck, shoulder, and down his arm. He inclines his head toward her, and then she's saying something into his ear that I can't hear.

Tearing my gaze away, I push down any sort of emotion that rises up in me. I can't be doing that in a room full of supernatural creatures who can read me like a book. But I know if they start making out, I'll be yelling 'bank is closed' and leaving as fast as my feet can carry me. Actually, that's not a bad idea.

"I'll be back," I announce, and then before anyone can stop me, I'm out the door and down the stairs. Now that I've officially made a fool out of myself...I need a distraction. I need a break from my thoughts and my worries.

If I let myself stop moving for even a second, the plethora of emotions will overwhelm me. I'm barely staying afloat as it is. I can't think about my dad, and I can't think about the plague. All it does is make me want to curl up on the floor and cry. I definitely cannot afford that at the moment. Even though I'm running on empty, I'm still running. I'll take what I can get at this point.

"Is the room not up to your standards?" Hector's voice pulls me out of my thoughts, and I look up to find him before me.

"It's great, th—" I stop myself before I can thank him. "I wanted a glass of water."

Hector nods before walking over to the bar with me on his heels. We've been eating nothing but granola bars and beef jerky since we left the school, and as the smell from the kitchen hits me, my stomach growls.

"Would you like dinner as well?" he asks, clearly not missing the sound. I shake my head, and he takes that at face value. After handing me a mug filled with water, I raise it slightly in the air and walk away. I'm not in the mood to talk to anyone, least of all a fae I'd have to be careful around.

As I walk through the hall, I pass a sitting room. There are plenty of creatures sitting in the main room, but this area is empty. Finding a spot by the window, I settle down and give myself a moment to feel.

I know I promised myself I wouldn't lose it in front of anyone, especially those upstairs, but here and now, alone in this room, I let a tear slip down my cheek. Only a moment, that's all I get, before I have to push my emotions down.

Somehow, I have to figure out how to help my dad. It feels like I've been searching for him forever, and now, there is finally a lead. My family and I were so sure the Ancients took him. He was doing research on them, trying to find something that would help us defeat them. He was on one of his recon missions to one of the covens when he disappeared, leaving all his stuff behind in his hotel room. Mother didn't feel his demise, so we presumed he was taken for something specific. Now I find out the fae had him, and I can't even pretend to guess as to why.

But somehow, someway, I will find a way to get him back. I'll have to get word to my family, but I'm not sure how that's happening anytime soon. Maybe once I'm in the castle, I'll have a chance.

So many things are happening at once, my head spins from thinking about it. I wipe at my tears, taking a deep breath. There's nothing for me to do but focus on one problem at a time. Getting back to the academy and warning them about the plague is the next order of business.

"Do you want to talk about it?"

I'm not even surprised.

I turn as Liam pushes away from the door frame and walks farther into the room.

"How long have you been there?"

"Not long. But I don't have to see you cry to know you're hurting." He takes a seat in front of me, and I reach over to take a swig of my water before I meet his eye.

"That was a stupid move on your part, Liam," I say because I want him to understand just how foolish it was. Not that it really matters. He'll always do what he deems best.

"I would do it again."

There it is. The expected response. I cock my head to the side, studying him carefully. It's always been true that he's different from the rest of the fae. Both he and his half-brother grew up away from this place, away from the rules of this world. He's always been kinder, softer, which makes it easy to forget he's one of them. But I'm seeing glimpses of it now. Ever since I got here, I've been seeing it more and more. Yet, it doesn't stop me from pushing him.

"Why?" I ask, because I need a good reason. What if Natalie never said anything to me? Aiden would be gone and so would Liam. I wouldn't even know where to look.

"Because you needed answers, and this was the only way to get them." The guilt I carry close to my heart rises up, but now is not the time. Instead, I push further.

"So what? Aiden and you are friends now?" The question isn't hostile exactly, but Liam doesn't miss the undercurrent in my words.

"I wouldn't go that far, Mads. But I also wouldn't let him go into that forest on his own."

"Because?"

"Because he would've gotten himself killed, and you would've been heartbroken."

I bristle at that immediately because Liam is not supposed to know about my confused feelings toward the shifter. No one is supposed to know. Well, besides Jade. But I know she wouldn't tell anyone.

"Come on, Mads. You should know better than to try and keep that from me. I know you."

And he does. Better than anyone in a long time, which is very surprising considering we've only been friends for a little over a year. But maybe it's true what my sisters always say. It doesn't matter how long you know someone, when you click, you click.

"It's not like that," I say anyway because how am I supposed to admit it to him when I refuse to admit it to myself?

"Mhhmm."

"Don't do that, Liam." I point a finger at him before I stand and being pacing around the room. "Don't make this into something it isn't."

"Just because it isn't doesn't mean it never will be."

At that, I spin toward him, amazed he would even say that. He would have to be blind not to see what's happening between Natalie and Aiden.

"They're promised to each other, Liam. I don't play into that equation."

"And yet, he broke the queen's rule and went into the forest for you. Actions speak louder than words, and all that." He shrugs, but I can't allow hope to blossom. Instead of encouraging this conversation any further, I walk over to Liam and sit down next to him. My head falls onto his shoulder as he reaches over and takes my hand.

"Please don't ever do that again," I whisper. I may be mad at him for keeping me out, but the fact that he could've been gone from my life forever overpowers that. I don't expect him to reply because anything he says will sound more like a contract. But then he squeezes my hand and warmth spreads up my fingertips.

"I won't."

THE NEXT MORNING, WE GET UP, EAT BREAKFAST, AND LEAVE without any extra flair. Some have given us weird looks, but we've mostly been left alone. I have to be thankful for small favors. Also, there haven't been any weird dreams. I'm not sure what to think of that. A part of me is glad and another part is worried. I'm not naive enough to think the queen doesn't have something up her sleeve when it comes to me.

The shifters went out and grabbed some supplies, replenishing what we brought, which means I haven't talked to anyone but Liam. Not that I'm complaining. The distance is good for me. Or it will be. I should get used to not being around a certain someone.

Aiden and Natalie stay to the front of our little group with enough distance between us that I couldn't hear what they're saying even if I wanted to. Which, of course, I don't. Liam walks to my right, Ben to my left, with Owen bringing up the rear. Somehow, I've ended up in the middle, as if they're protecting me from everyone around me. I don't know if I should be flattered or offended. I decide to take it at face value since I have other things to worry about.

We walk through the day with absolutely no issues. I thought the trolls would come back, but I haven't heard anything in the forest around us. The quiet makes it so much harder for me to stay out of my own head. I try to sift through the information in my mind, looking for answers. It's wishful thinking, but I would love for the library to suddenly be available to me now. There has to be something there I can use.

"Should we stop for the night?" Ben asks when the forest grows even darker. Since I'm the only one without extra special sight, the decision comes down to me.

"Let's stop," I say, keeping my eyes directed at Ben. No one questions me, and once the perimeter is set, everyone settles into their corners. Owen is taking first watch, and as I study my companions, I realize they're all feeling it. That foreboding hangs over us the closer we get to campus. It's not fair for me to think I'm the only one feeling all these emotions. They have friends there too, all of this affects them just like it affects me.

"Am I allowed to ask about it?" Ben takes a seat beside me, keeping his eyes trained on the trees. Since we left the village, he's been staying close, but we haven't really talked.

"There's nothing to talk about."

"You know that's not true." He turns, looking me straight in the eye. We have become friends through all this and for that I am thankful. But I can't spill my deepest and darkest to a beta. Especially to Aiden's beta. When I don't speak, he sighs. "I want you to know, Maddie," he begins, keeping his voice as low as possible, "What you did for him, for all of us, it was beyond impressive."

I smile at that and reach over to squeeze his forearm. He pats my hand and stands, understanding that's as much as I can give him at the moment. So much of me is exhausted. I feel as if the last week has lasted a year. Between the attacks, my own magic, and coming here, nothing is what I ever would've expected my life to be.

On their own, my eyes drift over to where Aiden and Natalie are sitting. She's been staying extra close to him, and I can understand that, even though I don't like it. She's his mate, and there's nothing to be done about that. When they move to lay down, I tear my gaze away and look up at the sky. Not much of it can be seen through the giant trees, but I pretend it's there.

I miss my family something fierce. Even though we're not looking at the same sky, I pull on the knowledge that they may be looking up as well. Harper and Bri are probably with their significant others, pouring over books and potions. Mama is probably with the council, researching more ways to keep the town safe. Right now, I wish I was with them. I wish I could talk to them and ask for their advice. My family means the world to me and being this far away from them, it's another weight I have to carry.

But then I think of my father, and the fact that he is under the same sky as I am. Somehow, I have to figure out a way to get to the

Winter Court. I'm more than aware of the tension between Spring and Winter, so I know better than to ask the queen for help. But maybe she can tell me something I can use. And maybe a certain other fae can be of help.

I glance over at Liam, and he looks up as if he feels my eyes on him. His eyes narrow, and I give him a small smile. He doesn't look reassured, but he doesn't press it. After the events of the past few days, I know better than ever that he has my back. That's what I'm going to focus on. I may not have my family here, but I have my friends. And they're as good a family as anyone can ask for.

20

The moment we step through the hedge, I know something is wrong.

The blanket of danger that's been hanging over our heads this whole time, suddenly covers us without preamble. We're surrounded on all sides. The shifters move to attack as I raise my hand.

"Stop!" I shout, freezing them in their tracks just as a guard steps forward. His uniform is custom tailored, the dark green adorned with gold thread. Before he speaks, I know what this is about.

"By the order of the Queen, Madison Hawthorne, you are to come with us immediately."

Nodding, I move toward him when Aiden's hand is suddenly on my arm. Turning, I find his eyes full of concern and caution.

"What are you doing?"

"I'm going with them."

"No, you're not."

That protective streak of his is much adored but also very frustrating. I shrug off his hold, receiving a slight growl.

"It's part of the deal, Aiden," I say, keeping my voice low but urgent.

"What deal?" he and Liam ask in unison as the fae takes a step toward me.

"The deal I made with the queen. Go back to the academy," I plead, hoping this once they listen to me. "Let Headmaster know what's happening, and see if you can find out more information."

"Miss Hawthorne." There's a hint of threat in the guard's voice as he says my name again.

"How many bargains did you make?" Aiden asks as I take a step away from them. Raising my eyes, I look him dead on, so he knows just how much I mean what I say next.

"As many as were necessary."

I turn then and rush to the guards before I say anything else. Especially something I'll regret later. A shout comes from over my shoulder, and I twist to see guards stepping from the side, grabbing my friends by their arms.

"What are you doing?" I yell, rushing toward them. But the leader of the guards has already grabbed me around the middle, and he's dragging me back. My magic flairs up as I watch Aiden and Liam being restrained, but right before I can let loose, heavy metal falls on my wrist, cutting off whatever I may have done. I glance down to find a shackle around my skin, and my magic freezes.

"Stay in line, Miss Hawthorne. Or someone will get hurt."

The last thing I see is Aiden's panicked look as the guards swallow me up and carry me to the castle. I wonder if I'll have to struggle for miles, but then a portal opens up and I'm pushed through.

When I land on the other side, the image of the group I left behind is still vivid in my mind. Even Liam looked scared, and that's not something I expect from him. Honestly, I probably should rethink my stance on everyone at this point. Liam looking worried is almost as weird as Aiden looking panicked.

"You better not hurt them," I snap, writhing my arms away from the guards holding them. The head guard steps forward again, a face full of disdain. He clearly thinks I'm below him, and I wonder if he'll strike me to keep me silent, but then he straightens and moves away. For the first time, I look around the room. I'm in a large office with bookshelves on each side. It's bigger than the last room I was in but similar. Then, my eyes land on the other person in the room.

Queen Amaryllis, ruler of the Spring Court, rises slowly to her feet and makes her way toward me. Everything about her is smooth and tailored to make her look regal. She looks like she's gliding across the floor, and for a moment, I wonder if she is. The fae often use their magic absentmindedly, and in a way that makes them one up each other. The queen is a master of that, as she would be.

"Your friends are fine," she says before taking a seat on a purple velvet armchair. It looks like it costs more than half the buildings in my hometown. The queen inclines her head toward a bench with a cushion, and the guard at my back pushes me forward. I glare over my shoulder as I take a seat. They really need to knock it off with manhandling me.

"Please tell your guards to stop pushing me around. I am perfectly capable of following directions on my own." The anger gives me a voice, and the queen's eyebrows raise a little at the tone. But I'm not backing down. I'm done being afraid. This won't end well for me if I don't stand up for myself. The queen waves her hand, and the guards melt away into the background. I guess that's as good as I'll get, but I'll take it.

"I am glad to see your journey was a success," she continues, and I wonder if that's really true. There's an underlying current to everything she says, and I wait for the other shoe to drop. "We can begin our partnership now."

And there it is. She may say partnership, but I'm not stupid enough to believe that.

"What is it you ask of me?" I already know I won't like the answer.

"You are to remain at the castle for as long as I require. We will begin magic exercises immediately. We must learn what we can about your...abilities."

All the words she's saying are pretty, but it still makes me feel like nothing more than a science experiment.

"And if I refuse?" I dare to ask, and the temperature in the room drops immediately.

"I would advise against it."

The threat has been given, and there's nothing I can do to protect myself except learn how to use my magic more effectively. Maybe there's a way I can use this for my own agenda; although, I know the queen won't hesitate to sacrifice me when the time comes. She needs me for a purpose, and the best way I can help myself and my friends is to learn what that is. Steeling myself against whatever may come, I look her right in the eye and say,

"When do we begin?"

BEING AWAY FROM EVERYONE HAS BEEN HARD. IT'S BEEN A WEEK, and all I've done is try to stay afloat without completely losing my mind.

Headmaster Marković came and visited earlier yesterday but could only stay for a few moments. He couldn't even talk to me without the watchful eyes of Queen's Guard lingering near. I've been assigned the captain of the guard, and he's been staying especially close. The queen called him Kurtis, but I doubt that's his true name.

I asked about my friends, and he said they're doing fine. There has been no sign of the plague the Oracle mentioned, but Headmaster isn't dismissing it. He knows better than anyone that what she says will come true. They've made preparations, and what I'm doing here, the training the queen is giving me...I hope it helps.

"Your Highness." I greet the queen as I step into the library. I wonder if I'll ever see past these few rooms. I go from my room to the library and once to the throne room. But that's it. Today Queen Amaryllis is wearing a bright pink dress, the brightest of colors I've seen on her. The sleeves are long and made up of sheer material, with patches of lace here and there. The skirt is full, but as she walks, I see there are slits all throughout. For some reason, the dress makes me think of Jade and with it comes a touch of sadness.

My own outfit consists of a dark blue, off the shoulder, embroidered dress. The neckline is v-shaped with long sheer puffy sleeves, and the skirt is layered with tulle. The queen has provided a wardrobe, even though I told her Jade could put together a bag for me. Queen Amaryllis wouldn't hear of it. She has a specific view of who I am, and nothing is going to change that.

I miss my jeans. In the sixteen years of my life, I've never worn so many dresses. They're beautiful, of course. The fae have a way with style. But they're not me, no matter how much the queen tries to make it so. The only aspect of my new wardrobe I do enjoy is the killer hooded cape. It makes me feel like Robin Hood or something.

"We will begin with a simple exercise," Queen Amaryllis says, and I turn to focus on her. She walks over to a large bowl in the middle of the room, and I come to stand beside it. "You know what to do."

I do because we've been starting every lesson with this exercise. Closing my eyes for a second, I find my center. My magic has seemed to replenish itself in the last few days, and I'm thankful. Ever since we came to Faery, I've been a little worried.

When I open my eyes, I raise my hand, and the water follows suit. It grows into a column in front of me as I watch the droplets sparkle in the afternoon light coming through the window. Twisting my hand at the wrist, I let my fingers flutter up and down, and the water moves with them. I've come to do this exercise whenever I'm around liquid. It soothes me in an unexpected way, like stretching a muscle after sitting in one spot for too long.

"Multiply it."

Bringing my other hand up, I pull the water apart, spreading it into a long line, hand length across. I haven't been able to create animals or objects like I did by the river, but the water listens to me more than ever before. With my left hand, I throw the droplets into the air, and as they fly, they become a sky full of stars. The other half of the water hangs in an orb over my right hand. As I hold the droplets over my head, I turn to the orb. Calling forth a little more of my magic, I watch as the orb grows in size, doubling almost immediately. Then, I swing my left arm, pulling all the droplets from the air and slamming them into the orb. The water explodes as it comes together, and I mold it into a pillar once again, before it can get anything wet.

"Now, use your words."

At first, I want to protest. We've tried it once before, and it made me so tired, I couldn't think straight for the rest of the day. But this is why I'm here. I don't want to find out what she'll do if I resist.

"What are you asking me to do?" I ask instead, hoping for more direction. That's the thing about lessons with Queen Amaryllis. She's not really teaching me anything. She watches as I practice my magic and then demands I do certain types of spells. What I wouldn't give to have someone who understood my story spell casting explain to me exactly what it means and how it works. Instead, I'm making up my own rules.

"Multiply it."

Great. She just expects me to know my onions. It's frustrating, and it's infuriating, and it's— I take a calming breath before I do something I'll regret. Turning my focus back to the pillar of water still holding strong in front of me, I think back to the river. I felt my magic explore itself, like it was growing and blossoming on its own. Maybe I can replicate that here, without too much of the story spell casting magic. It's worth a try.

"You move and you grow,
You tumble and you flow,
But with words you'll come before,

And dance like flowers after snow."

The part of my magic that I keep under lock and key bangs on the walls, desperate to get out. But I do my best to push it back, to keep it contained. My words bring the water higher and higher before it splits into a meadow full of flowers. The moment the blooms open, a pain sharper than any I've felt before doubles me over. The magic boils hotter. It spreads throughout my body like it's demanding to be felt. I yelp, unable to contain myself, and I thrust my arms in front of me, pushing them toward the water. The rush is instantaneous, and my head spins with the feel of the magic pouring out of me.

I scream as I try to reel it in, but it won't listen. The water multiplies by ten and then it bursts in every direction, covering every surface and pushing all the furniture against the wall. The pain resides, and I drop to my knees, breathing heavily.

"Now, pull it all back." The queen speaks up, and I glance over to find her completely dry while I'm drenched. I didn't have enough power to protect myself from the blast, but she clearly did.

"I can't."

"You will."

There's no kindness in her gaze, just cold command. Knowing I can't refuse her, I reach for the water with my right hand, calling it to me. At first, there's a moment of resistance, like a petulant child who doesn't want to come inside after playing with his friends, but then it drags its feet toward me. I hold steady, my whole body filled with exhaustion, but I don't stop until every single drop is in the bowl. The volume of water diminishes, and it's only what we started with. Unable to stand on my feet, I stay on all fours, my head spinning.

"That's a start," the queen says and walks out of the room.

✨ 21 ✨

W hen a knock sounds on the door, I jump. I'm not exactly expecting any visitors. After my water disaster a few days ago, the queen has continued to push me, but my magic hasn't been responding as well. Yesterday, she announced there would be no lessons today because I am required to attend a celebration. Hours after getting up, I'm still trying to figure out what I'm supposed to wear to this ball. Or why it's so necessary that I go.

"I'm coming!" I call out when the knocking becomes insistent. Pulling the door open, I gasp before I'm swallowed up in a tight hug.

"What are you doing here?" My voice is mumbled as my friend holds me tight.

"I'm here to get ready for the ball!" Jade replies, pulling back and giving me a once over. "You look good, by the way. I had these nightmare-esque thoughts that they were starving you or something."

I laugh, my first real one in a week, and reach for her again. It feels so good to be held by someone kind. Not that I'm being held by anyone, and that's the problem.

"But how?" I lead her farther into my room as she gazes

around. She's as impressed as I was, but she doesn't comment. She knows me well enough to know that any kind of praise for this place will not sit well with me right now.

"Headmaster Marković requested it. We're all required to go to this ball anyway, so he just made sure I could come get ready with you."

I don't even want to know how he managed that. But the headmaster has been around for a lot longer than I can imagine, so it's not like he'd be making dumb mistakes when it comes to the fae.

"Did you bring anything to wear? I have nothing here but the clothes they've provided."

"Which looks amazing on you," Jade comments, giving my yellow dress another look. The queen seems to enjoy me in yellow, even though I've never been a fan of the color for myself. It's really more of my sister Harper's color. But it's as if the fae royalty want to make sure I'm as far from myself as I can be while I reside in this castle.

"Thanks, but—"

Another knock sounds on the door, but this time, whoever is on the other side doesn't pause. Three fae walk in carrying various items including two large boxes. They place the items on the bed, turn, and walk out without a word.

"That was strange," Jade comments as the door shuts behind them.

"Actually, that's pretty normal," I reply, walking over to the bed. After popping the lid off the box with my name on it, my breath catches. The material inside is made of the night sky, full of stars and magic. As I pull the dress out, it grows in size until it's a full gown, falling around me with flair.

"Wow, Maddie. That's...gorgeous," Jade whispers, the look on her face full of awe. I walk over to the mirror, holding the dress up to me, and I have to agree. The shoulders are bare, with quarter sleeves running down the arms. The skirt is full, with a layer of mesh and lace over it that seems to move on its own. The desire to wear it right this minute is almost overwhelming, but I push it away. Putting it on will be the last thing I do before we go to the ball.

I turn just in time to watch Jade pull her dress out of the box. It's dark pink, and it complements her complexion perfectly. The sleeves are long, and there are jewels all over the outer layer.

"I'm supposed to wear this?" Jade asks, completely amazed.

"That's the plan."

After we lay our dresses out on the bed, I go through the rest of the items that were brought over. There are shoes, hair oils, and makeup.

"Wait, is that mine?" Jade grabs the bag, and I realize it is. They went into our rooms and brought us our own hygiene items. I'm not complaining about that part, just the part where they were in our space. Not that we truly have our own anything while we're in Faery.

"Please tell me how you've been," I say, sitting down in front of the mirror with my makeup bag in hand. I only use a few items from it usually, but tonight, I want to match the intensity of the dress.

"It's been strange, Maddie," Jade begins as she settles on the bench beside me. The mirror is large enough for the both of us, and I'm grateful for small favors. "Everyone is on high alert even though no one has mentioned any real danger. We still have classes like nothing is happening, and the teachers are trying to keep a smile on their faces, but we can see they're strained. It's like there's something they're not telling us."

I keep my face as neutral as possible because if the headmaster decided not to tell the school about the plague, I won't be doing so either. Aiden and his pack are good at keeping secrets, so I didn't expect there to be any leaks in the information. The thought of him makes me pause as I reach to apply eyeliner. I've been working so hard to not think about him.

"Vera is mostly back to her old self, although still a little more private," Jade continues, and I force myself to focus on her words.

"Noel and I have been spending extra time together. I do like him; I just don't know if now is the right time."

That doesn't sit well with me, and I turn to Jade immediately.

"You can't wait for the perfect time," I say, my words coming out a little more forcefully than I intended. I dial down immediately. "I mean, you don't know what tomorrow holds. You guys are great together. I don't want you to miss out on something just because you're afraid of what could be."

She's silent for a moment as she studies me. It's difficult not to fidget under her scrutiny. But it's as if she's working up to say something I won't want to hear.

"Like you and Aiden?" she finally asks, and I shake my head immediately.

"Aiden and I are nothing like that. We have no future beside the trainer/student relationship we've been in. You and Noel are more than that."

"I don't think that's true, Maddie, and neither do you. Not the Noel part," she hurries on to add, reading the situation and where I was going to take it perfectly. "There's more to you and Aiden."

"Maybe on my part. But he—"

"He went to the forbidden forest for you," she interrupts. "I may not know everything that happened, but I know he made a bargain to help you. That's way more than just trainer/student."

I realize if that's all she knows, then she doesn't know about my father. There's a part of me that wants to dwell on her words, but I can't think about Aiden and what he means to me.

"He's been a moody mess since the queen took you. He's raged about it on more than one occasion. The pack have all been walking on eggshells around him."

"Jade, please stop," I whisper, not able to take any more of it. How I feel about the shifter is almost overwhelming. I can't allow myself a glimpse of hope because I know it won't do me any good. It'll just hurt so much more in the end.

"I'm not saying this to be cruel, Maddie." She reaches over, wrapping me in a side hug. "I just don't want you to regret not going after something that was important to you because you were afraid."

Well, she basically just threw my words back at me, but I'm not mad at her. She's right, and I'd be a hypocrite to say otherwise. But no matter how much I don't want it to be true, Aiden is promised to another. That's something I have to come to terms with before I ruin my heart forever.

"Jade, there's something I have to tell you." I say instead, knowing she needs to hear this from me. I won't tell her about the plague, not yet. But I will tell her my other secret.

"What is it, Maddie?"

"I know where my father is."

๑๛๑

A FEW HOURS LATER, JADE AND I ARE SITTING IN THE CHAIRS near the fireplace, both of us adorned in our gowns. The feel of the silky material against my skin is the purest form of pleasure. I keep running my hand over my stomach, mesmerized by the way the material twinkles. It's like there are actual stars on my midnight blue dress. We've talked about my dad, but mostly, it was me sharing memories of him.

"I feel like I understand you a little better," Jade comments with a small smile. "You'll get him back."

Before I can say anything, a knock on the door comes right before it opens. Kurtis, the head of my protection detail, steps through as Jade and I stand.

"I have come to escort you to the ballroom," he says, giving me a quick once over. While there is usually cool detachment in his gaze, this time, a spark of something almost close to approval comes over him before he's back to his stoic self.

"Jade, this is Kurtis. My personal warden." I smile sweetly, knowing just how much he hates it when I call him that. Or use his name so flippantly. While I know it's not his true name, the fae guard that more than life, it makes me feel better not calling him guard.

"Wow, he seems cheery," Jade comments as we follow him out of the room and down the stairs.

"He's a ball of laughs," I reply to his back, but he's too used to me now to even bother turning around. Not that I ever get under his skin. He's as cold as they come. When we finally reach the outer doors to the ballroom, I pause.

"Are you okay?" Jade asks, bringing Kurtis' attention to us. He doesn't look happy, but he also doesn't push me immediately into the room.

"I'm nervous. I haven't seen anyone in over a week now." My breath catches as I try to breathe and calm my nerves. A chill comes over my naked shoulders, traveling down my arms and spine. The dress has quarter sleeves, but I'm still cold all of a sudden.

"You look amazing, and everyone is eager to see you," Jade comments, reaching over and taking one of my hands in hers. "Let's do this."

I smile gratefully and grip her hand tightly. It used to be that I was the brave one, but apparently, I've lost some of my edge. Kurtis pushes the doors open, motioning us inside. For some reason, he showed me this small kindness and I'm thankful. I give him a quick nod and then Jade and I are inside.

The room is huge, much larger than what it looks like from the outside. I'll never get over the underhanded way the magic works here. The ceiling has chandeliers that twinkle, the walls are adorned with murals and live vines blossoming with flowers. The queen stands on the other side of the floor, and as I look over, Kurtis takes his place beside her. Both of their heads are turned in our direction, and even though I can't meet her eye, I know she sees me. I incline my head in greeting, and she answers in kind before she lifts her hand and waves it in my direction. The magic reaches me instantly, and I try to figure out what she did.

"Maddie, your skin," Jade whispers, her voice full of awe. I glance down at my arms and find them covered in tiny glitter. Jade pulls out a small mirror from her pocket, because both of our dresses have them, and I look to find my cheeks and lips are covered in it as well. I look...ethereal. The queen gives me another nod as I glance at her, and this time, I return it with a little smile. I still have no idea why she's treating me this way, but for this one moment, I'll accept it.

Tables are set up on the outer perimeter, and there is dancing happening in front of the throne. Already, the room is filled with laughter and talking. The fae love their parties, and this one is no different. When I hear my name called, I spin around in time to be lifted straight off the floor by two strong arms.

"Ben, put me down!" I laugh, feeling like myself immediately. "You have got to stop doing that."

"Never!" he replies immediately before sobering up. "Unless you mean it. Then I'll stop."

"No." I squeeze his forearm reassuringly. "Never stop." He grins in response, and my heart fills with warmth at the sight of him. I've missed him.

"Move over, shifter," I hear and then Vera steps around Ben and is reaching for me as well. I hug her, then Noel, and everything seems to fall into place.

"Castle life has been good to you," Vera comments, looking at my dress and face.

"Today has been a good day," I reply, as vague as possible. I don't exactly want the queen to overhear me talking bad about this place. Not that she doesn't know I hate being here. "Let's dance!"

I'm soaking up every single second of the time I have with my friends, and I will do it to the fullness of my ability. Vera and Jade both grab my arms, and we stumble onto the dance floor. The music is louder in this part of the room, kept so by magic, no doubt. This isn't a typical ball that I've read about where everyone is dancing the same waltz. This is a place where everyone lets the music guide them, and that's exactly what we do. The boys join us, and as I bump into Ben, he lifts me and spins me around. My eyes catch on Owen who's watching from his position against the wall, and he smiles at me, almost making me stumble. He won't join us, but he's happy to see me.

Music gets louder as the voices rise up, and I don't care what I look like as I get lost in the moment. Because if I don't let myself go, I'll be too focused on the fact that Aiden is nowhere in sight.

22

The Spring Court sure knows how to party. My head is spinning from all the dancing and laughing. There's a sheen of sweat over my skin, and it only makes me glow in the low light. I haven't felt this much myself since before the Ancients came into the picture. It's as if all my worries have been stripped away. It's just me, my friends, and a world of possibilities.

Our group stumbles over to the nearest table, sweat dripping down our backs, laughing loudly. Well, Jade, Noel, and I are a little sweaty. The shifters regulate their temperature much better. Even so, when I wipe at my face, none of the glitter comes off, and at the moment, I'm thankful. I've felt the queen's eyes on me for most of the evening, but she hasn't asked me to approach. Thankfully.

"I'll be right back," I almost shout into Jade's ear as I push past the throng of people toward the closest door. My skin buzzes with adrenaline, my heart beating a mile a minute. When I glance back, my friends are all laughing, and it brings a smile to my own face. I push through the doors, almost tripping over my own feet, and the instant quiet hits me immediately. There's a magic in that as well as I look back past the threshold and into the ballroom. The contrast is staggering. Being out here in the quiet, my mind instantly clears.

I take a deep breath, turning to study my surroundings. The hallway opens up in three directions, with the party at my back. Surprisingly, Kurtis hasn't followed me out, but I doubt I'm truly on my own. The queen has eyes everywhere, and I don't want to make things worse for myself by wandering somewhere I shouldn't be. But then I realize this area looks familiar, and my feet move before I even tell them to.

Walking over to my right, I come to a set of doors I've seen before. Without a second thought, I push them open, and the fresh air hits my flushed cheeks. I realize I'm in the small garden Aiden and I rushed through barely two weeks ago. The thought instantly makes my heart heavy, and I curse him for not being at the ball. I have no idea how he got away with it, maybe he's on patrol, but even though I know it would hurt me, I still want to see him.

Now that my head is cleared and my skin is less flushed, I feel more like myself. Even my magic seems more settled inside me, as if it needed this little reprieve as much as I did. I walk over to the nearest bench, settling myself on it slowly. Arranging the dress around me, I lean back, looking up at the night sky. It seems there are way more stars in this realm than at home, and the thought is bittersweet.

"It's strange, isn't it?"

His voice reaches me right before he steps out of the shadows. I should know better than to be surprised. Somehow, he always finds me. My heart leaps at the sight of him, the messy dark hair, the dark suit he wears. The top button of his dark blue shirt is unbuttoned, and it somehow makes him look even better.

"What is?" I ask as Aiden makes his way toward me. He takes a seat beside me, and I curl my hands, fisting the material of my dress to keep myself from reaching for him. Maybe some of my inhibitions are still lowered because it's a harder battle than it should be.

"How beautiful this place is but also how deadly."

I glance at him out of the corner of my eye and find him already watching me. Now that he's close, I can tell just how tired he looks. Underneath all this glitter, I carry the same bags under my eyes. My heart squeezes for him, and the desire to fall into his arms intensifies.

"Would you like to dance?" he asks suddenly, completely disarming my defenses. Aiden stands, placing his hand in front of me like a proper gentleman, and against all my internal alarms, I reach for it. His skin feels like heaven as his fingers wrap around mine, and he pulls me to my feet. Aiden's other hand slides across my back, pulling me against him as much as the dress allows. Even though I'm wearing wedges, he seems taller somehow. He begins to guide us in a simple waltz, something we all learn very early on in our covens. It's tradition, and he seems to be just as skilled in it. We don't need music, as we move to the rhythm of our hearts. The hearts that are beating in sync.

I thought I knew magic. I thought I understood the physics behind it. But now, I realize I've never known true magic until my heart is one with Aiden's, and we're gliding across the paved ground under the moonlight.

As if we're both overwhelmed by what we're feeling, we stop, and I raise my head to look into his eyes. There's a storm brewing there, and I feel my own eyes answer in kind. It's so hard to keep myself from moving closer, from closing the small space between us and finally knowing what he tastes like on my lips. His eyes flash, as if he can read my mind, and my skin flushes hotter. There's only one way I can stop this, and even though I hate myself for it, I ask the question anyway.

"Where's Natalie?"

Aiden narrows his eyes, not missing my tactic. Maybe it'd be better if I put some distance between us, but it's like I can't move away.

"Is that really what you want to know?" he replies, his gaze unyielding.

"It doesn't matter what I want," I say before I can stop myself. He spreads his hand out on my back, and I move just a fraction closer to him.

"Why doesn't it?" he asks, and we both know this is a dangerous game to play. Every time we've ended up here, it hasn't ended well for either of us.

"Have you found a way to stop the plague?" I ask my next question in the arsenal of dodging-the-issue-at-hand questions. A small chuckle escapes him at that, and I fight the urge to smile.

"It's always business with you, Duchess," he comments, finally releasing me from his hold. Yet, I still don't move.

"Someone has to keep an eye on the ball," I fire back, which earns me another chuckle.

"If you weren't wearing that dress, we'd see just how committed you are to keeping your eye on the ball."

That makes me stop. "What is that supposed to mean?"

"It means we haven't had a training session in days. Who's to say you can even handle yourself anymore." There's a gleam in his eye that I'm not used to. That's when something dawns on me. His inhibitions are lowered too. He's acting like Ben and Vera, freer than I've seen them in, well, ever.

"Aiden, I think the party may be affecting you."

"Maybe. Or maybe I'm just saying all the things I've been holding back."

I freeze as he comes close again, his breath washing over my cheeks. He raises his hand, running his fingertips over my cheek, a complete look of awe on his face.

"You look like magic," he whispers, filling my chest with so much emotion, I think it's going to choke me. "You always look like magic."

"Aiden." But he doesn't seem to hear me as he continues.

"The kind of magic that takes your breath away, but it's also unattainable. Like something from another world." His hand moves over to my hair, holding a strand between two fingers as he plays with it almost absentmindedly. "The first time I saw you, you took my breath away."

My emotions are beyond torn. I want to stop him, to keep him from saying something he'll regret later. But the selfish part of me, it wants to know what he truly thinks of me.

"You hated me on sight."

"I hated that you mesmerized me, and I could never have you."

Tears well up in my eyes at the raw emotion in his voice. I can't stop myself from reaching for him. I take his face into my hands, a palm at each cheek, as I pull his attention to me.

"You have no idea what that means to me," I say, trying to keep my tears at bay. Maybe if he doesn't remember this, I can show him a glimpse of my own feelings as well. "You will always have a place in my heart. But you need to let me go now. You're not your-self. You don't know what you're saying."

"My mind has never been clearer," he replies, shaking off my hands from his face and taking them into their own. He holds them over his heart, the heat from his skin sending pleasant sparks up my arms. "I am bound by duty, but my heart belongs—"

He doesn't get to finish his sentence as the screaming begins.

I RACE INTO THE BALLROOM WITH AIDEN ON MY HEELS. THE sense of urgency has seemed to clear his mind enough to go fully on alert. We stop right inside the doors, a scene like something out of a horror movie opening up in front of us.

Every creature, fae, shifters, and witches alike, are screaming and writhing on the floor. About half of them are throwing up blood while the others are trying to help. My eyes search for my friends, but I can't see them.

"Aiden, where's your pack?" I ask, turning to the shifter beside me. He narrows his eyes, using his supernatural sight to see some-thing I might not, and then he's reaching for my hand.

"Come on."

He leads me through the throng of people, his grip firm on my hand. A sea of bodies opens up in front of us and there they are. My eyes immediately land on the body on the floor and then I'm the one pulling Aiden behind me. Dropping to my knees, I slide right up to my friend, reaching for her. But before I can touch her, Aiden is there, wrapping his arms around my waist and pulling me away.

"Don't touch her!"

"Let me help her!" I scream, trying to get out of his tight grip. Jade doubles over with pain before she turns to her side and vomits blood. Vera, who's the closest to her, jumps back, completely horrified.

"We don't know how this spreads. You can't help her if you get sick too," Aiden hisses into my ear, and I go slack in his arms immediately. Getting in her blood would be the surest way to get sick, if we aren't already.

"Where's Noel?" I ask Vera as I look around me once more.

"He went to get a drink with Owen. Then this started, and—" She trails off, looking lost. Not that I blame her. I think at this point, Aiden's arms are the only thing holding me together. I give myself another second before I turn and look him in the eye.

"You can let go now. I'm okay."

He doesn't do so immediately, as if afraid if he does, I'll fall apart. Or disappear. Then, after a firm nod, he releases me, and I find my footing. Every part of me wants to reach for Jade, but I don't. I have to be smart about this.

Glancing up, I look for the queen. I know she was here when we first came in, but now she's gone. Probably ushered to her chambers for safety. I see some of the teachers on the floor as well, but no headmaster. Or any of the Elders. Granted, I haven't seen them since the first day we got here. Some of the guards who are not sick have begun giving orders, trying to keep everyone under control, but it's not doing much.

"We need to get her out of here. And find the rest of our friends." Aiden nods before he walks over to the closest table and rips the tablecloth from it, shattering the dishes. Then, he walks back over to Jade, careful not to get into any of the blood. Placing the tablecloths over her, he lifts her into his arms, and I reach over to cover her face as well.

"You'll be okay, Jade. We'll make sure of it."

We turn to go with Vera behind us, and I still don't see Noel or Ben or Owen anywhere. But there are so many creatures around, I can hardly see the walls. I'll have to use my magic to get us out of here, but when I raise my hand to call on it, a loud boom sounds throughout the room. Jade is lifted right out of Aiden's arms, and before either one of us can do anything about it, we blink and we're no longer in the room.

Twisting around, I find that we've all been transported into the throne room. Well, all the healthy creatures at least. The throne is empty, but then the noise brings my attention to the balcony, and I see the queen stand.

"It seems a plague has come into our court," she says, her voice clearly heard by every single creature in the room. "The sick are to be kept in the ballroom, quarantined for the time being, as we search the cause of this sickness." There are murmurs all around, but all she has to do is clear her throat and everyone falls silent. "Leave and return to your rooms and houses. Interactions between other individuals are to be kept to a minimum."

Just like that, everyone disperses. I turn to Vera, her eyes huge and filled with worry and fear.

"Get back to the academy," I say, giving her a comforting smile. "I'm sure the headmaster will have more information for you there."

"You can't come with me?"

"I can't."

We embrace then, even though we're not supposed to be touching, and she follows the rest of the student body out the door. Aiden doesn't move, staying as close to me as possible as the room empties out. I'm hoping he forgot our exchange, even though I will never be able to. But that's just another burden I will bear for the both of us.

"Go find your pack," I say, hoping they're okay. I couldn't see if they were in the room or not, so I still have hope.

"What about you?"

I look over my shoulder and find the queen's eyes on me.

"I have to get back to my room," I reply, turning back to Aiden. He studies me for a tense moment, and it's like he wants to say something, but at the last moment changes his mind.

"I'll come see you the moment I can," he says before turning on his heels and sprinting for the door.

I watch his retreating back and then, once again, I'm all alone.

23

Before I can take two steps in any direction, Kurtis is there. I don't even ask why, just motion for him to lead the way. The castle staff moves around me in a control frenzy as the quarantine is put into place. I wish there was a way I could see if the rest of my friends are in that room, but when the queen summons, I don't say no.

"Madison Hawthorne, your prediction seems to have come true," the queen greets me as I step into her chambers. I've never been in here before. We usually keep our lessons to the library or the gardens. This room is larger than any I've been in, besides the throne and the ballroom. Her bed sits to one side and could probably fit a dozen people easily. Everything is adorned in throws and there are pillows on every surface made for sitting. The fireplace is on the other side of the room, and it's taller than I am. The gold design almost blinds me as I do a quick scan. This is definitely a room fit for a queen.

"Not my prediction, Your Highness." I feel inclined to point out. I never quite know how much I can get away with when talking to her, but I'm not about to take ownership of what happened in that room. My heart squeezes just thinking of my friends and the rest of the students who have gotten sick.

"Maybe not, but you brought the message to me, and now it is here." Her eyes are cold as she watches me, and that's when I realize what she means.

"I didn't make this happen. You said you can feel my magic. Have I used it?"

Her eyes narrow, but she doesn't answer right away. I glance over at Kurtis, but as usual, I can't tell what he's thinking. I can't let myself forget in how much danger I am constantly in. But right now, the worry overpowers everything.

"You have not," the queen finally answers, and I breathe a little easier. I need to be more careful. I know that. "Now, you will."

"What?"

"You will write a story to cleanse my court of this illness. And only my court." At first, the words don't register.

"I can't," I stammer, looking at the queen as if she's lost her mind. Not even two days ago we had an exercise that went poorly, and now she wants me to use my magic on people.

"This was not a request," the queen states, her cold stare going right through me. I understand what she wants, but I'm not ready for that kind of magic. I've been exhausted for days after the last exercise. A part of me is not even sure I'll be able to do it. Even if I wanted to, which I absolutely don't.

"My magic is weak, it wouldn't work."

"Your magic may be weak but only because you refuse to use the proper channels. Do not think I do not know you have been trying to substitute your Hawthorne water magic for the story spell casting. I can read you like a book."

"Then why let me?" I raise my voice, throwing my hands in the air. "Why am I even here? My spell brought us to Faery, and I am sorry I have messed up your way of life, but all I want is to get back to my school and to my world. Why keep me here?"

"Because you are valuable!" Queen Amaryllis' voice booms around me, shaking the walls. Her eyes flash, and I can taste the raw power of her magic. "You are a tool, and I will use whatever means necessary to ensure my court is the last one standing. If you want to keep your precious school safe, then you will do as I command."

My body shakes as she speaks, from anger or fear, I can no longer tell. A million things rush through my mind, but I can't seem to articulate any of them. It doesn't matter anyway because she's not done.

"You have till tomorrow morning to speak your decision. Go!"

With that, she turns and leaves the room while Kurtis steps forward. I put up my hand, stopping him from reaching for me. But I realize I have no idea how to get to my room from this part of the castle, since I've never been here before. So instead of storming out of the room, I wait for Kurtis to lead the way. I'm surprised to find my room is actually quite close to the queen's chambers, only two hallways away. But maybe, I shouldn't be surprised at all. She has me here for a reason.

When I step through the doorway, the door shuts at my back with a slam. Alone for the first time, I drop to my knees, hiding my face in my hands. The plethora of emotions overcome me all at once, and I find it difficult to take in a full breath. Tears smear my mascara as I cry for everything that has happened and everyone who got hurt.

My heart bursts with pain as I think of Jade. I have no idea who else is sick, and I'm afraid that when I do find out, it will already be too late. If I could write a story spell to wipe it all away, I would. But I'm not strong enough to do something so...risky. Because the last time I tried, I brought us to Faery. What if I try to erase the sickness and instead erase my friends?

The sadness is quickly replaced by anger, and I get to my feet only to grab the closest thing to me and fling it across the room. There's a thud as the decorative pillow hits the wall but I'm not done. I kick at the chairs, turning them over as I fling a tapestry off the wall. I wish I could punch something. I wish I could stop being so useless. The rage builds and builds until I can't take it anymore. I drop down to all fours, not sure what I'm going to do. But then, something stops me.

⚜

WHEN THE KNOCK SOUNDS, IT'S SO FAINT I BARELY HEAR IT. Then, it comes a little more insistently, making me sit up. I glance at the door and listen, but when the third knock sounds, it's not coming from the door.

Quickly, I jump off the floor and hurry to the window. Pulling the curtains back, I gasp as Aiden smirks at me through the glass. I unlatch the lock, swinging the window open, and Aiden lands softly on his feet right inside my room.

Since I'm on an upper floor, the queen didn't deem it necessary to lock the windows like she locks the doors. Which I am truly grateful for at the moment.

"How did you..." I begin to ask when Aiden places a finger to his lips and motions toward the door. Before I know what to do, the shifter dives under my bed just as the door swings open, and Kurtis walks in.

"Can I help you with something?" I ask, not disguising the annoyance in my voice. Kurtis' eyes swing to the open window, and he marches over to it to look out. "Hello?"

"Why is this open?"

"Because I needed some fresh air," I snap, placing my hands on my hips. It takes serious self-control not to glance at my bed and make sure Aiden is hidden. But I trust him to take care of himself, at least in this situation. Kurtis gives me a suspicious look before pulling the window closed and latching it again.

"Leave it until the morning. You need to go to bed," he commands. He motions toward my dress, and I realize I haven't changed after the ball. Quickly, I reach for my nightgown, holding it in front of me, but Kurtis doesn't move. Annoyed and a little terrified he'll search my room further, I step behind the changing curtain and quickly strip and put on the nightgown.

When I step out, Kurtis hasn't moved. He gives me a quick once over and then marches out the door. I stay in my spot, not daring to even breathe for fear of giving something away, even after the door is closed. It's another few seconds before Aiden stands in front of me.

"That answers that then," he comments, giving my room a once over.

"What?"

"I wondered if the windows had a magical alarm system like the doors. It seems so."

Truth be told, I'm not surprised. The queen watches me like a hawk. I guess it's too much to ask for her to trust me with an open window.

"Is he always like that?" Aiden nods toward the closed door. I cross my arms in front of me, realizing I'm wearing little besides this cloth.

"Basically." That doesn't sit well with the shifter, so I hurry to change the subject. "What are you doing here?"

"I told you I'd come see you as soon as I could." He shrugs as he proceeds to walk around the room. I follow his line of sight, trying to see this place from his point of view. It might seem glamorous, and yes, it is, but it's still a prison. A prison made up of pretty walls. And a little messy from my earlier outburst.

"What have you found out?" I ask, not sure what to do with myself now that we're alone in my room. I realize it's been weeks since we've spent any time together like this. Not that I'd tell him, but I miss our training sessions.

"Noel and Ben are both sick."

His words squeeze at my heart, and I shake my head, as if I can make the truth disappear. Walking over to the chair in front of the fireplace, I sit, my emotions high.

"Owen?"

"He's fine."

"Natalie?" I almost don't ask, but I have to know.

"She's sick."

"I'm sorry." And I am. No one deserves what they're going through. It seems I'm continuously helpless to do something about it. Unless I do what the queen commands. "She wants me to write a spell."

"No!" The outburst surprises me. I look over at Aiden, and the fear in his eyes, before he manages to mask it.

"What do you know?" I lean forward, my full attention on him. He looks away, as if he said something he shouldn't have. "Aiden."

"Liam and I talked about..."

"About me."

"Yes." He turns to face me again, leaning forward as well. "He said story casting is dangerous. It...it takes something from the storyteller."

"What?"

"Part of you. Part of your story."

The words slam into me, making the room spin even though I'm sitting down. Aiden is kneeling in front of me in a flash, his eyes full of concern. For someone who guards his emotions so carefully, he's letting me see too much.

"What does that mean exactly?" I whisper, staring at the flames over Aiden's head.

"He doesn't know. He just knows it will steal parts of you and your magic. Every time you cast."

I guess it makes sense if I think about it. Liam was so worried about me after I brought the academy here. And after, he kept asking about my magic. It's true that it took longer for it to replenish itself, and that's not something I've experienced before. But everything seems to have gone back to normal.

"The queen has commanded me to story cast the sickness out of her court. And only out of her court. She wants to use it as a battle tactic."

Aiden and I stare at each other, realizing at the same time the amount of magic that would take. The toll it would have on me.

"I don't know how to get out of it," I say, honestly. She let me go tonight, but tomorrow, she'll be back to demand her spell, and there's nothing I'll be able to do about it.

"We'll figure it out," Aiden says, bringing my attention back to him. He takes my hands in his, holding them on my lap. This is the side of him I've only seen once. He's gentler with me than he's ever been, and it brings tears to my eyes. "We'll figure it out," he says again, and I nod, swallowing the sadness. This is no place or time for such frivolous emotion. But his kindness disarms me, and I don't know what to do about that.

I lean back, closing my eyes because it's harder for the tears to leak through. Aiden gives my hands a gentle squeeze before I feel him moving away. I've taken the coward's way out. The moment could've turned into something, but it's not something we could come back from. Well, not something my heart would be able to recover from.

It's been days since I've slept well, but with Aiden here, I feel safe for the first time in forever.

"Will you stay?" I ask without opening my eyes. It's safer this way, at least for me.

"I don't think I have much of a choice." I roll my head to the side, meeting his eyes briefly before I close mine once more. He's right of course. If I open the window again, Kurtis will come back, and I doubt Aiden would be able to get away. "When was the last time you slept?" the shifter asks, and I smile.

"I don't know. I haven't felt safe enough to really try."

Maybe it's my tired brain talking because I don't mean to reveal that much. At least I'm not looking at him, so I can't see what he thinks of my small confession.

"You can rest easy, Duchess." His voice is soft, and it's like the first drops of rain on my heated skin. I've come to love that nickname, even though I don't agree with it. "I'll keep watch."

Settling a little more comfortably in my chair, I smile without opening my eyes.

"Tell me a story."

I'm not sure what possesses me to ask, but the words are out, and Aiden surprises me once more when he complies.

"Did you know that when I was a young wolf, I was terrified of witches."

"You? I can't imagine you scared of anything." I chuckle, already being lulled into slumber with the sound of his voice. There's a small pause before he speaks again.

"You'd be surprised." I want to comment on that, but I'm already fading. "There wasn't a coven anywhere nearby, so I grew up with a very skewed view of witches. The first time I met one, she was angry at my father for something and came barreling down toward us with wind flying all around her. She looked enraged, and I shifted immediately and hid behind my dad. My dad made up with her, and she ended up being a babysitter of sorts anytime he needed to go into the city."

There's sweetness in his memory, and I can hear the smile in his voice. The next thing I know, strong arms are lifting me up, and I barely open my eyes to find my body cradled against a strong chest.

"You're buff," I say to his chest and feel him chuckle. "And brave," I mumble as I feel myself being placed carefully on soft sheets. The presence of him beside me makes me feel invincible, so when he moves to go, I grab his arm and pull him onto the bed beside me.

"No, stay. Safe."

He chuckles again but doesn't move away, just stretches out beside me. My eyes open just a crack, and I find myself looking up at him. Satisfied, I let my eyes drift shut and snuggle deeper into the covers.

"Strong and brave," I mumble. "Protector." Silence greets me, and soon, I'm back in dreamland. But through the fog, I hear a gentle whisper.

"If you only knew how terrified I am when I'm around you."

24

When I wake up, something is missing. My hand runs over the space beside me, and maybe I dreamed being curled up against Aiden in the night. But then I hear a noise. I glance over to see him tending to the fire, and I know I didn't. He stayed with me, and he held me while I slept. It was the first fully restful night in ages.

"How did you sleep?" he asks when he sees that I'm awake, and I stretch my hands over my head before I reply.

"I actually slept, which says a lot."

"I'm glad."

We stare at each other, a new kind of intensity between us, and I don't know what to say or do. Do I say thank you? Or do I ignore the fact that I overheard him confessing how scared he is around me? Instead, the decision is made for me when I hear the clock chime.

"Oh no," I say, jumping off the bed. "You have to get out of here before they find you."

I hurry over to my closet and pull out one of the dresses the queen has given me. When I turn, Aiden is standing in the middle of the room, staring at me. Electricity sparks between us, and if I could bottle it up, it would make my magic seem like child's play.

"Go, Aiden. Before you get in trouble."

He nods, moving to the window. After another searing look at me, he reaches for the latch.

"Promise you won't spell cast," he says when I join him at the window.

"I'll do my best," I reply before yanking the window open. He jumps from the ledge without a word and hurries off. When he's out of sight, I pull the nightgown over my head just as the door opens at my back, and Kurtis walks in.

"Maybe knock!" I exclaim appalled as I pull the dress in front of me. Not that he cares, since he's fae, and they run around naked sometimes. Just for fun. For some reason though, he gives me the decency of turning around, and I hurry to pull the dress over my shoulders. Once I'm done, I close the window and walk over to the mirror to pull my hair back into a ponytail. I'm not about those fancy hairdos, that's for sure. I'd rather leave it down, but if I'm to fight battles today, I need to look ready for one.

"Are you ready to begin?" the queen asks when I step into her chambers. I frown, confused at her tone.

"I thought I had time to decide."

"We both know what you're going to decide," the queen replies, walking over to the large window and looking out. There's something so unnerving about seeing her this nonchalant. Her court is in grave danger, and she seems to not have a care in the world. Treading carefully is a must when it comes to her, but I already decided to be firm.

"Then maybe we don't have the same idea of what that is."

Her laugh surprises me, sending a chill down my spine. There is always a sense of otherworldliness about her in the way she moves and the way she speaks. But at this moment, there's a touch more of it, and it turns my blood cold.

"You are an interesting creature, Madison Hawthorne. So much raw power, so untapped." She turns to me then before she waves her hand, and the doors on the opposite side of the room open up.

She walks through, and when Kurtis almost pushes me in, I follow. It seems to be a portal directly to her throne room. It's why I've never seen her walk the hallways. She doesn't have to.

Once there, I'm surprised to find the room empty. I'm not sure what I was expecting, but maybe something to convince me to do the spell. The queen walks over to her throne, taking a seat as if nothing is the matter. She doesn't speak, and I don't volunteer either. We stay like that for a few very tense minutes, but I have no idea what she's doing.

"You really do not want to help your friends?" she finally asks, turning her full attention to me. Today, she's wearing a deep green dress, and the gold crown on her head seems more intimidating than ever before.

"Of course I want to help my friends."

"Hmm, yet, here we are. If you do not cleanse my court, and only my court, you cannot save your friends."

The threat is evident, and I'd be stupid not to heed to it. But I don't know how to do what she asks and not lose myself in the process. My magic is already unstable, and after what Aiden told me, there isn't a way for me to do what she wants and not hurt myself in the process.

"Your Highness." I have to make her understand. "My magic is unconventional and confusing. I need more information. Maybe if you let me go back to the academy, the teachers there would be able to help me find out more about it. Maybe then I can—"

"You think they know more than me?" she snaps, cutting off my plea. "You do not learn from those who do not understand."

Confusion clouds my mind as I try to figure out what she means. How could they not understand? And why would she? Forgetting all protocol, I have no choice but to call her out on it. If I'm punished for disrespecting her, then so be it. I need answers.

"You have never explained to me why you decided to teach me." I stand up a little straighter, hoping my voice sounds as confident as I wish it to. "You basically imprisoned me within these

VALIA LIND

walls and made me play with my magic in front of you and never gave me an ounce of direction. How can I learn if you don't actually teach me? How can you understand if this magic is so rare?"

Her eyes flash, and for a moment, I think she'll strike me dead right here and right now. But then she leans forward, her complete attention on me, and I feel her magic rising up inside of her.

"Silly child, no one has ever been truthful with you, have they?" What an odd question, but I don't get a chance to comment as she continues. "Story spell casting is as ancient as the creatures waking up all over the world. The evil that brought you to my doorstep is the same evil that created what is inside of you."

"I don't...I don't understand."

"Story spell casting has been around since the world began, and it was first spoken by the Ancients. I know it because I too possess a pinch of it. Not as powerful as you, of course. It is not my main magic. That is reserved for the Ancients."

At first, I don't think I hear her right. What she is saying can't be true. But fae can't lie.

"No, that's not possible. I can't be...evil."

Her laugh rings out all around me, sending a chill down my spine.

"You are not evil, child," she says. "But you can be. With the right direction."

That's what she's been trying to do? She's been molding me in her own way, and I haven't even realized it. I wonder if anything we've done helped her cause, but how would I even be able to tell?

"I see the horror on your face. It is a sight to behold." The queen smiles, and there is no kindness there. "Now, I believe you need an extra motivator."

She flicks her hand and the doors to the left open. My heart drops in my chest as two guards walk in, dragging a body between them.

"Aiden!"

I move toward him, but my feet won't cooperate. Glancing at the queen I find her hand raised, holding me in place. Aiden is dumped at the foot of the throne, and I can't do anything but watch. He raises his head slightly, and I can barely see him through the tears pooling in my eyes.

"What game are you playing?!" I scream at the queen as I fight against my magical restraints. She leans back on her throne, flipping hair over her shoulder as she grins at me once more.

"Does it really matter? I intend to win."

❀

"Why can't you understand that I don't know what you want me to do?" I yell, straining against my invisible restraints. The queen flicks her hand again, and Aiden screams, his body twisting with agony. "Stop, just stop!"

I'm showing all my cards, but I can't bear to see him like this. There are cuts all over his body, as if he's been whipped repeatedly. He has shackles over one of his wrists, and I recognize them as the ones they used on me to keep my magic dormant. Aiden can't shift, and if he can't shift, he heals much slower.

"You do know what to do," the queen says, leaning to one side as she watches me. "It is buried deep in your blood. All you have to do is reach for it."

"I don't know how!"

"You do."

Another wave of the hand and Aiden is lifted straight up before being slammed to the ground. My throat is hoarse from all the screaming, and I can't see well through the tears. It feels like my heart is split in two, and it's bleeding all over the place. Aiden grunts, rolling over to the side. At first, I think one of his arms is broken, but then, he moves it, opening his eyes and looking up at me.

"I'm okay," he mumbles over the blood pooling in his mouth, and I can't take it anymore. His words burn through me, and I scream, thrusting my hands in his direction. My magic leaves me with the speed of a bullet. Before it can reach Aiden, it dissipates. I look up at the queen as she narrows her eyes at me.

"That is not the magic I am looking for." She curls her hand into a fist, and Aiden jerks in pain again.

There's annoyance in her voice now, and I can see her growing impatient with every moment I don't deliver what she wants. A part of me can't even understand why she doesn't do something herself. She has plenty of magic, and yet, she wants mine. Just then, a guard rushes into the room, and the queen snaps her attention away from Aiden.

"Your Highness." The guard bows as the queen raises her hand, this time in the direction of the guard. "The general has requested your presence immediately."

The general? The queen stands, retracting her arm and magic from the guard. Her cold exterior doesn't change, but something tells me she's not happy with the turn of events.

"Take them to the dungeon while I deal with this mess," Queen Amaryllis says, descending the stairs and walking out the room without another glance at me. Kurtis waves his hand, and the guards surround us, grabbing me by the arm with a familiar shackle clicking into place over my wrist.

"What's happening?" I ask my guard, but he ignores me. They drag us out the throne room and toward a door at the back of the hallway. Without much fanfare, I'm half carried down the stairs before they deposit me on the cold floor. They're a lot less gentle with Aiden, and as he lands beside me, I crawl over to him. "Jerk," I mumble, glaring daggers at Kurtis. He gives me one of his steady looks before he shuts the bars and leaves us behind.

"Aiden, can you hear me?" I ask as I turn him over and cradle his head on my knees. When he looks up at me, it takes me a moment to collect myself. He looks even worse up close. "I'm sorry. I'm so sorry you're in this mess because of me." I place my forehead against his, the tears running down my cheeks and into his hair. A feather of a touch on my elbow brings my attention up,

OF DESTINY AND ILLUSIONS

and I look over to see him reaching for me. He pulls me down as I hold him close, wishing there was a way I could take it all away.

"Don't cry, Duchess," he says, his words a little muffled by his bruised face. "I'll be good as new as soon as I shift."

"You shouldn't even be here," I reply, raising my head to look at him. "What happened?"

"They grabbed me as soon as I stepped into the forest," Aiden replies before he moves to sit up. I guide him up, and we scoot enough that his back is against the cell's wall. "It's like they knew I would there."

"She's always one step ahead." I shake my head, frustration burning in my veins. "No matter how hard I try, I can't win against her."

"You didn't do the spell."

"No. I would've. When I saw you..." I stop, swallowing hard. "I don't know what she wants from me, and she keeps saying that I do, which makes me even more confused." I need my family. I need them to be here so we can figure this out together. But I feel a million worlds apart from them. No one is coming to save me. I have to do that myself. But I have no idea how. We stay like that for a while, and then, when I can't hold them in anymore, the tears come again.

"Hey." Aiden reaches over, wiping another escaped tear off my cheek. "We'll get through this."

"Don't be nice to me," I reply, hiccuping over my tears. "It confuses me."

He smiles then, or tries to, and it breaks my heart all over again. I will never understand the magic I feel when I'm around him, will never be able to explain how we got here, but it's like he's my person and that's where it starts and ends. He must see a change in my eyes because he cups my face, bringing it closer.

"Let me try something," I say, getting to my knees and reaching for his shackle. He nods, giving me permission to do whatever I'm about to do. Closing my eyes, I search for that energy within me.

With my own shackle over my wrist, I'm not sure if this will work, but I have to try. I can't stand the sight of him so broken.

Opening my eyes, I wrap my hands around the metal, and it heats up under my touch immediately. Aiden looks up surprised, but I shake my head. I need to concentrate.

> *"Things that are closed must be opened,*
> *And that which was padlocked must be unlatched.*
> *These are the rules that I have spoken,*
> *And they are to be obeyed and done."*

The metal shakes under my hands and then, it snaps open. Aiden glances at me as I grin tiredly, even that much magic took something from me.

"You shouldn't have—"

"Shift, Aiden. Just shift," I interrupt, and as I watch, he does.

His wolf is more beautiful than I remember. As I slouch against the wall, he moves toward me, nuzzling against my hand. Smiling, I run my hand over the soft fur on his face, then down his back. As I lean forward, he changes back to human and our faces are only inches apart. His face is clean of all cuts and the color is back in his eyes.

We watch each other with a new kind of an awe, saying a hundred things without any of them being spoken. His hand reaches for my cheek once more, and I lean into it, needing the feel of him against my skin.

"Can I kiss you?" His whisper washes over my flushed face, and time itself seems to stop.

"I insist that you do," I reply, right before his lips crush over mine. There is no awkwardness of a first kiss, no fumble of hands. We fit together as if we've been made for each other, and it's a special kind of magic all on its own. I pull him close, wrapping my arms round his neck, as he picks me up and places me on his lap. We're hungry for each other, and I'm not sure which one of us is the predator and which one is the prey. All I know is that I never want to stop kissing him.

"You seem to have found your motivation." A voice sounds at my back, and I pull away to watch Kurtis step into the light. "Now, we should probably be going."

25

"What are you talking about?" I ask, standing up and facing Kurtis straight on. Aiden rises beside me, a steady presence at my back. My skin feels hot, and I'm probably blushing, but I need to push all that away and focus on the situation at hand.

Kurtis doesn't answer right away but walks over and unlocks the cell's door. Stepping inside, he motions me forward, pointing to the shackle around my wrist.

"May I?"

I'm so surprised, I don't question him. He takes the shackle, unlocking it with a key, before he walks back over to the doors.

"We need to go. Now."

"I don't understand."

"Quick recap. I'm getting you out of here. Since you used your magic, the queen will think you did it on your own. She feels you using the magic, she doesn't know how much. So, let's get you back to the academy before she realizes something is amiss."

"Why?" I have to know. I don't trust anyone but the boy beside me right now.

"Because you can help us defeat the Ancients. But you can't do it if the queen is using you as her own puppet. There are much greater stakes involved here." He glances up, as if he hears something we don't. "We need to go."

I glance at Aiden, gauging his reaction. He looks at Kurtis before looking back at me. Then he nods, and I take that at face value.

"Lead the way," I say, motioning Kurtis forward. We follow him out the door and up the stairs. At the top, he motions for us to wait as he steps into the hallway. Aiden presses close beside me, and it's difficult not to look at him and think of what we just did. That kiss was made for storybooks, and I feel it in every part of me. I think I always will.

Aiden's gaze is as heated as my skin. He looks down, and I see him reaching for my hand. He holds his own out, as if asking for permission. Without hesitation, I place my own in it. The moment our skin touches, sparks shoot up my arm and over my body.

"Let's go," Kurtis says, popping back in, and we don't hesitate to follow him out.

"Where's the queen?" I ask, keeping my voice low.

"The Ancients have reached Faery," Kurtis replies, keeping his movements swift as we rush down the hallway. "There have been battles all across our lands for weeks, but now, the plague has weakened our defenses, and the Ancients are ready to take their place as rulers."

"I thought they wanted to destroy," I say as Kurtis pulls a door open, and suddenly, we're outside.

"They want to cleanse. Your world will fall first, then Faery. Then all the other worlds in between. They're powerful and hungry. Faery is the one place where magic is not diluted. They're taking its power from it."

"They did that in Hawthorne," I realize, thinking back to what my family has told me. Being here, I was so focused on my own problems, I forgot there's a magical war going on.

"How does Maddie play into that?" Aiden asks as Kurtis stops at the outer wall of the castle grounds.

"Your story spell casting is part of the puzzle. It's powerful magic, and it's as old as time. The queen wants to strike a bargain with the Ancients. If you write a story for her, one they cannot get out of, she will gain their favor and protection. She's been looking for it for a long time, and you've been on her radar. It's always about power, and you have a good chunk of it."

I let that sink in, realizing that maybe us ending up here wasn't so much only my doing. If she's been looking for my exact type of magic, it could've affected my spell without me even realizing it.

"Why are you really helping us?"

Kurtis moves his hands over the wall and then a door appears. He pulls it open, and the forest greets us on the other side.

"Liam wasn't the only one to grow up outside of this place," the fae guard finally says, a bit of sadness entering his voice. "I've done some terrible things to prove my worth to the queen, but I don't regret the choices I've made if it means saving the world I left behind. "

For some reason, I don't think he means just the world. He left someone behind, and the fae, they live for hundreds of years, and their memory lives on even longer.

"I appreciate what you have done," I say as Aiden ducks through the door. Kurtis nods but doesn't say anything else. I wish I had time to ask him all the questions I want to ask. But I don't. As Aiden and I run into the woods, the door shuts behind us.

My head spins with all the information we've learned, but my heart is heavy for the people we left behind. Our sick friends are still in there, and I just hope Kurtis stays out of the queen's way. I can't have anyone else on my conscience.

"We need to hurry. If he's right, the queen is already looking for us," Aiden says when I pause. But something is amiss, I can feel it in my bones.

"Aiden, wait," I say, pulling him to a complete stop. The forest is dark around us, even though I think it's still early in the day. I don't know how long we've been in the dungeon, but it couldn't have been that long. The feel of danger hangs low in the air, but as I look around, I don't see anything.

"What is it?" the shifter whispers, his eyes on my face.

"I'm not sure. Something is coming."

We exchange a look and then I let Aiden lead me toward the academy. Everything is happening at once. I have no idea if I'll be able to handle it, or if Kurtis got us out for nothing.

WE RACE THROUGH THE FOREST WITH AIDEN LEADING THE WAY. My head feels a little light, but it's better than what I expected after the use of my magic. In fact, the lightness is more of a buzz. As if I'm getting a power up instead of a drainage. Nothing is what it seems and everything about my life stopped making sense a long time ago.

The queen knew about me. Somehow, someway, she knew about me. I can't stop thinking that maybe I didn't ruin everything with my spell. Maybe it was always supposed to go this way.

"We're almost there," Aiden says after about ten minutes of weaving around the trees. He said we had to take the long way, just in case, and I trust his judgement. He hasn't let go of my hand since he took it. Not that thinking about that kiss is appropriate right now, but I can't shake it. I don't want to shake it.

"What are we going to do when we get there?" I ask a few minutes later when Aiden pauses.

"Go to Headmaster?" he replies, giving me a quick smile. "Whatever it is, we'll figure it out. Let's go."

I nod, and then we burst through the trees. The school looms in front of us, and the sight makes my heart leap with joy. I never thought I'd be this happy to see the academy. There's help to be found there and hope. We can save our friends; I just know it.

However, before we're even halfway across the lawn, that feeling of danger overpowers me and then I'm lifted into the air. Aiden is ripped away from me right before we're slammed into the ground. Disoriented, I push to my feet, my head spinning from the impact. Aiden gets to his feet as well, and then he growls, his attention on something over my shoulder.

I turn slowly to find Queen Amaryllis and her guards walking slowly out of the forest. My eyes narrow, but I don't see Kurtis with them, and I wonder what that means for the guard. The man that walks beside the queen now looks about fifty years old, with silver hair and an outfit full of armor. This must be the general.

"Aiden, get inside."

"What? I'm not leaving you."

"Please, this is between me and her."

"No." He grabs my hands, spinning me around to face him. "I stand by your side. Always."

Looking at him now, I wonder how I was ever going to survive not being with him. I know that's still on the table. After all, he's promised to another. But the fact that he cares, the fact that he's there for me, it makes all the difference. But I won't let him get hurt. Not again. I reach for the magic inside of me, and it answers happily.

"I'm sorry," I say, receiving a confused look, right before I push the magic at Aiden. Water rushes out of the ground, picking him off his feet and carrying him right into the school's front doors. He lands on all fours and jumps up quickly. The panicked look in his eye is evident, even from this far away, but I'm done putting those I care about in danger. He moves forward, but I slam the water and the doors, shutting them in his face.

"This door locks and keeps him safe," I mumble, hoping that's enough to keep the academy on lockdown.

"Someone is feeling a little more powerful," the queen says, broadcasting her voice toward me. I turn slowly, the energy of the water magic running all through me. I've been so afraid of what this can do to me and to my loved ones, I forgot the part where it can save them. Breaking that shackle didn't feel like a chore. It felt natural and easy. Not something the queen or the headmaster was making me do, but something I wanted to do.

"I'm not helping you," I say, knowing she can hear me. "I'm

done being a puppet. For you, for the academy. I'm in control of my own magic."

"What changed?" the queen asks, and I think she's genuinely curious. She couldn't break me with her exercises and her threats. I found my center all on my own.

"I did," I say, a smile splitting my lips.

That doesn't sit well with her. She raises her arms, and with them, roots spring up from the ground, racing toward me. I focus on the moisture all around me, and just like that, I feel it everywhere. Thrusting my arms in front of me, the moisture flies toward me and turns at my shoulders, racing toward the queen. The thorns and water clash, sending a small earthquake through the meadow. The guards stumble while the queen and I stay upright.

"Why are you doing this?" I shout as I pull up a wall of water between me and the queen. There's so much hatred on her face, it shocks me into stillness. That's all it takes. One of her roots get through, sweeping me off my feet. I drop to the ground, but I don't let go of my magic. The magic and me are one.

"I will not be played for a fool," the queen roars, sending another wave of her magic toward me. I block it, my battle and water magic merging together for a stronger shield. I think I hear shouts coming from behind me, but I'm not turning away from the issue at a hand.

"You want me to help you defend the Ancients, I can. But you can't hold me and my friends prisoner."

"I want your magic, you fool. I do not need you to save me."

But she does. No matter how much she talks, that's all it is. I realize she's worried. Worried that her court will not withstand, that she will be the one to fall. She was working to make my magic take pieces of me until there was nothing left. Until she could take my magic. It's like a rubber band snapping into place. Everything seems to make sense, and I don't know where the clarity is coming from, but I'm grateful for it.

Embrace your heritage. Embrace those who have come before you.

It's like there is a voice speaking directly in my mind. I realize that's what I've been missing. Connection. My magic connected to the story spell casting which connected to the history it carries with it. Maybe that's where this sudden knowledge is coming from, from those who've come before me. But I know what to do.

I still my heart and think of my friends and my family. The queen is shouting orders, and I feel her magic pulling at my water shield. The guards are running toward me, ready to take me down, but I don't move. I find my center and I speak.

"When Winter leaves, Spring takes its place,
When snow melts, flowers grow in its footprints.
There is no power stronger than that of love,
There is no story more interesting than of us."

I glance back at the academy, at the faces pressed against the glass as they watch helplessly. I find Aiden, the look of fear and rage on his face, and I smile.

"A girl learned a secret; she carried it in her heart,
She worried, and fretted, and hid,
So, no one would be the wiser and they would never be torn apart.
But a queen found a loophole,
And tore at the seams.
The girl learned another secret, but still, nothing was as it seems.
But that time has come for the words to be spoken.
And the girl, she's no longer afraid or broken.
She found herself and the secrets within,
She's more than she seems and so are they.
Her home is a place, but it's also a people.
And the queen is not welcome, nor is she able
To break through the bonds of love and friendship.
To destroy the sanctuary the girl is creating.
The girl says, Leave! And the queen obeys.
This is now her place and she is the one who holds the keys."

My head is thrown back as I utter the last word, and then my body feels like it's being torn apart. I scream as light and water twirls around me like a tornado and then, just when I think I can't take it anymore, it bursts from me, sweeping across the meadow and the school. There are screams, but I can't see past my own magic. And then, just as suddenly as it began, it stops. I'm lowered gently to the ground. Then, it's just me and the queen in the meadow.

I can see she's struggling with some unseen force as it pushes her away from me and from the school.

"This is not over," she shouts, anger dripping from every word. "Your friends are still within the castle walls. You have nowhere to go and nowhere to hide."

"I'm not hiding," I reply, projecting my voice loud and clear. "I will get my friends back, and I will heal them. But you are no longer welcome here, and you will never control me again."

With that, the queen's strength seems to give out, and she flies back into the woods before I can even blink. My bravado leaves me the moment she's gone, and I drop to my knees, trying to catch my breath. There's still a buzz over my skin, and I am attuned to every water molecule in the area. Breathing deeply, I try to calm my racing heart.

Aiden is suddenly there, followed by Liam, as they reach for me. Aiden sweeps me into his arms, while Liam takes one and holds it tightly.

"That was some magic, Mads," Liam says, a bit of awe in his voice.

"I think, we haven't seen anything yet," I try to smile, but then sleep takes me away.

FIVE DAYS LATER I'M IN THE HEADMASTER'S OFFICE, LOOKING out the window. I still haven't been able to find a way to get my friends out of the castle. The queen has sent word to the headmaster saying the plague has taken lives, but that's all we know. I don't even know if my friends are alive.

I'm trying not to think about them, or my father. If I let myself dwell on all the things I can't control and all the people I can't save, I become useless.

"Have you had any luck with your research?" The headmaster asks from his position behind the table. In the last few days, I've learned that the Elders were able to escape before the queen put a lock on the portal, and the headmaster hasn't been able to speak with anyone from our world. He and the teachers have been doing their best to keep the students in line, but it's getting harder by the minute.

"No. I still can't get in."

I've tried the library a dozen times, but even with my more focused magic, something is preventing me from entering. So, the boys and I have started pouring over every book we can find within these walls. We've read through a lot of what the headmaster carries in his office, and we're no closer to any answers.

"You will figure it out, Miss Hawthorne. I have no doubt."

"That makes one of us," I mumble as I head for the door. We've been having these early morning check-ins, and I'm not sure they're doing me any good. It's just a reminder of everything I haven't accomplished. Even though there's probably more he'd like to say to me, he doesn't stop me when I leave.

As I walk the halls, everyone is so much more subdued. The fae who weren't originally enrolled in the school have all gone after the spell I cast. As far as I know, only the original students remain. Plus, Liam. I trust him, so I guess my magic caught on to that.

The kids know about half of what's going on, but no one tries to stop me as I head toward the back doors. The teachers are doing their best to try to keep moral high, but even though there are still classes, they've been reformatted for our current situation. More battle training, more potion creation. We're getting a crash course in our heritage because all of us will need to know how to fight if we're to get back to our own world.

My feet carry me across the grass and to the outer building I know so well. Since the academy became a sanctuary, and I took a five-hour nap after casting the spell, my combat training has been in full swing and slightly modified.

"You sure about this?" Liam says in greeting as I walk into the room. Aiden turns at his words, his eyes finding me immediately. We haven't talked about our kiss, or all the little ways we told each other about our feelings. But there's a new kind of an intensity whenever I'm around him, and I feel him so much more, even when I'm not with him.

"I need all the skills I can get on my side," I reply with a shrug.

"Very well."

Liam hands me a sword, and I take it with both hands. Even after we started combat training, I never thought we'd resort to swords. But this is the weapon of choice in the magical community, and it's the one that can inflict the most damage. That's what I'm looking for. Aiden and Liam are both skilled, so they're the perfect people to teach me.

As Liam talks me through the basics, my gaze keeps jumping to Aiden. A part of me is glad we're not alone. We haven't been since we were locked in the cell together. But the other part wants him all to myself, and I know he feels the same. That awareness that has always been present is more intense than ever. Sometimes I find myself catching my breath because being near him is so overwhelming.

"Aiden will attack, and you will block." Liam's voice instructs, and I force myself to focus. The shifter comes to stand in front of me as I grip my sword a little tighter.

"Don't tense so much," he says, and his voice does funny things to my stomach. "Move into the motions, don't force them."

I nod, and he attacks. He swings his sword overhead, and I raise both of my arms to block. He does it again, and I block again. He's not putting all his strength into the swing and still, each one vibrates my body. Liam moves to the side, giving us the floor as Aiden and I dance around each other.

To some degree, he's still angry at me for locking him inside the academy. But I think to the other, he understands. It's the alpha in him that wants to do the protecting, but that's my job now. No matter what happens, he will always have me watching his back. Maybe one day, I'll be able to tell him. Maybe one day, I'll be able to tell him just how much he means to me.

"Good. Now—" He trails off, catching himself and I narrow my eyes. "We're going—"

"Aiden?"

He leans on the sword, his other hand at his chest. That's when I notice he's a lot more sweaty than usual, droplets of it running down his temples and down his neck.

"We need—"

Suddenly, he drops to his knees, and I'm at his side in the next moment.

"Aiden?" I reach for him, cradling his head on my knees as he convulses under my touch. I blink the tears away as I try to hold him together. "No, Aiden. No."

"Mads, let go of him." Liam is there, trying to pull me away, but I won't go.

"No!" I scream, tearing myself out of his grip. "We have to help him. He's just—"

"He's got the plague." I know Liam says the words, but they don't register.

"He's fine. He's just tired. He's okay." My words tumble over each other as I wipe at his face. The shakes stop, and then start up again, and he rolls to the side, vomiting up blood.

"Maddie."

"No, he's okay!"

I don't even care if I'm getting blood all over me, I hold him close as his body shudders once again, and then he goes still.

MADDIE'S LIST OF OLD SLANG WORDS/PHRASES

"Bank is closed!" - what you say to someone to stop making out

Berries - denotes that something is good, desirable or pleasing.

Dumb Dora - an unintelligent woman

Mrs. Grundy - an uptight or very straight-laced individual

"Know your onions" - to know what's up or what's going on

Source: thoughtcatalog.com

NOTE FROM THE AUTHOR

Thank you for reading my book! If you have enjoyed it, please consider leaving a review. Reviews are like gold to authors and are a huge help!

They help authors get more visibility, and help readers make a decision!

And if you'd like to know what comes next, sign up for my newsletter! More books are coming!

http://eepurl.com/ioJC5

Thank you!

NEXT IN THE THUNDERBIRD ACADEMY SERIES

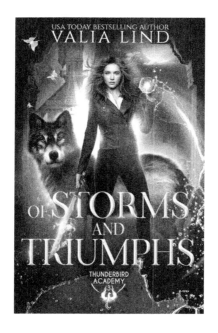

Coming March 2020!!

Preorder today: Of Storms and Triumphs

All I had to do was write one spell to save us—instead, I doomed us all.

Stuck in Faery, with her friends in mortal danger, Maddie has no choice but to push herself beyond her limits. Her magic is growing, but so are the secrets behind it.

Will she be able to save them? Or has she ruined her chances in redeeming herself?

This is it. The final battle. The last chance to save those she loves.

Full of magic, adventure, and romance, Of Storms and Triumphs is the final book in an addicting young adult paranormal romance series by USA Today bestselling author Valia Lind that will keep you reading late into the night!

Click here to preorder today!

ABOUT THE AUTHOR

USA Today bestselling author. Photographer. Artist. Born and raised in St. Petersburg, Russia, Valia Lind has always had a love for the written word. She wrote her first published book on the bathroom floor of her dormitory, while procrastinating to study for her college classes. Upon graduation, she has moved her writing to more respectable places, and has found her voice in Young Adult fiction. Her YA thriller, Pieces of Revenge is the recipient of the 2015 Moonbeam Children's Book Award.

Sign up to receive a text for new releases and sales!
- https://slkt.io/C6B
or text VLindBooks to 31996

ALSO BY VALIA LIND

Hawthorne Chronicles - Season One
Guardian Witch (Hawthorne Chronicles, #1)
Witch's Fire (Hawthorne Chronicles, #2)
Witch's Heart (Hawthorne Chronicles, #3)
Tempest Witch (Hawthorne Chronicles, #4)
The Complete Season One Box Set

Hawthorne Chronicles - Season Two
Of Water and Moonlight (Thunderbird Academy, #1)
Of Destiny and Illusions (Thunderbird Academy, #2)
Of Storms and Triumphs (Thunderbird Academy, #3) - Coming March 2020!

The Skazka Chronicles
Remembering Majyk (The Skazka Chronicles, #1)
Majyk Reborn (The Skazka Chronicles, #2)
The Faithful Soldier (The Skazka Chronicles, #2.5)
Majyk Reclaimed (The Skazka Chronicles, #3)
Complete Box Set

Havenwood Falls (PNR standalone)
Predestined

The Titanium Trilogy
Pieces of Revenge (Titanium, #1)
Scarred by Vengeance (Titanium, #2)
Ruined in Retribution (Titanium, #3)

Complete Box Set

Falling Duology
Falling by Design
Edge of Falling